SAVING SCOUT

Charon MC
Book 5

KHLOE WREN

Books by Khloe Wren

ISBN: 978-0-6483085-0-8
Copyright © Khloe Wren 2018

Cover Credits:
Models: Darrin James Dedmon
Photographer: Golden Czermak of Furious Fotog
Digital Artist: Khloe Wren

Editing Credits:
Editor: Carolyn Depew of Write Right

Acknowledgements

As always, I have to give a massive shout out to my wonderfully patient husband. Who continues to put up with his insane author wife. And to my girls, as once again this book saw me locked away in my writing cave more often than not.

As always, I couldn't have written this book without all the help I received with my research. In particular Nicole, Maggie and Dawn.

To the Night Writers Facebook group. Our bond has been tested these past months as we've lost two of our own, but the unwavering support I find with you all is such a blessing in my life that I appreciate more than you know.

To my Facebook street team, Khloe's Kickass Bikers, Beasties and Babes, thank you for your support and help. Thanks ladies!

To all my friends who helped me get back up each time I stumbled while writing this book. Liz Iavorschi (my heart still hurts), Dorothy Shaw, Tracie Runge, Eden Bradley, Elle Boon, Miranda, Dawn and Tamsin Baker, you ladies especially.

To my editor, Carolyn, no matter what I throw at you, you always come through with a marvelous edit. I appreciate everything you do and thank you for another job well done.

To Darrin and Golden, thank you for the awesome image that is PERFECT for Scout.

Finally, a huge thanks to Maranda and Jo Carol for beta reading for me this round.

xo

Khloe Wren

Biography

Khloe Wren grew up in the Adelaide Hills before her parents moved the family to country South Australia when she was a teen. A few years later, Khloe moved to Melbourne which was where she got her first taste of big city living.

After a few years living in the big city, she missed the fresh air and space of country living so returned to rural South Australia. Khloe currently lives in the Murraylands with her incredibly patient husband, two strong willed young daughters, an energetic dog and two curious cats.

As a child Khloe often had temporary tattoos all over her arms. When she got her first job at 19, she was at the local tattooist in the blink of an eye to get her first real tattoo. Khloe now has four, two taking up much of her back.

While Khloe doesn't ride a bike herself, she loves riding pillion behind her husband on the rare occasion they get to go out without their daughters.

Dedication

For Liz Iavorschi,

Much of this book was written in writing sprints with you by my side, writing your own books. It's been a week since I learned of your passing, and I still can't quite wrap my head around the fact you're gone.

Rest in peace, my friend.

Charon:

Char·on \ˈsher-ən, ˈker-ən, -än\

In Greek mythology, the Charon is the ferryman who takes the dead across either the river Styx or Acheron, depending on whether the soul's destination is the Elysian Fields or Hades.

Prologue

21ˢᵗ March 1992

Marie

As I fought and screamed at the two men who were trying to pin me down, I wondered why the hell I'd been so excited to come to this damn place. When Sarah had scored us an invite to a party at the infamous Iron Hammers MC clubhouse, we'd both thought we were so cool. At eighteen we were going to go have our first taste of adult freedom. No foster parents to stop us from having a drink, or anything else we wanted to do or try. Everyone knew you could get whatever you wanted at the Iron Hammers MC clubhouse.

It had all sounded so good in theory, but I should have known better than to believe it was going to be all sunshine and rainbows.

The moment I was on the ground, I was pinned down with my arms out flat. I felt the prick of a needle at my inner elbow, then everything went foggy on me. My limbs grew heavy, like someone had tied weights to my hands and feet... Why was I pissed off again? I couldn't remember, but I knew I was angry for some reason. I frowned as I tried to figure out what had happened.

"Fuck, I hate the ones who fight. Put these two in the back of the room, they'll need a few doses before they'll be any good to fuck."

Unable to make any sense of his words, I grinned up at him. Suddenly, I was feeling *very* friendly, but it seemed I couldn't talk. My dry mouth refused to move. Maybe I needed a drink. My gaze landed back on the man who'd spoken. He was kinda hot in a rough, biker way. I scrunched up my nose when he picked me up and I landed over his shoulder. He needed a shower, and I needed a bucket. At the first retch, he threw me down onto a mattress and rolled me to my side so my face was in a bucket. Eww. I hated being sick. Once I was done, he released me and I flopped back onto the mattress. I had a really good, happy, buzz going on, and I hoped it wasn't going to fade anytime soon.

I was only kind of tracking what was going on around me when my shirt and bra were suddenly gone and rough hands began tugging at my bare breasts and nipples. At the jolts of pain I tried to push the hands away. It was interrupting my high, but my arms were so heavy I couldn't be sure I managed to move them, especially with the way my eyes were playing tricks on me. A deep chuckle filled my ears, too loud. I winced and groaned as I rolled away.

"Yeah, another shot or two and you'll be so much more fun, bitch. I'm looking forward to breaking you in."

His words floated in and out of my haze-filled mind but I didn't really understand them. Nothing mattered. Only this blissful happy place I was in, that I could enjoy now he'd quit hurting me.

Sometime later, my brain started to track what was going on around me. Grunts and groans of men having sex filled the room along with feminine whimpers. Where was I? What the fuck had happened? Carefully, I opened my eyes and when all I saw was blank wall, I rolled so I faced the other way. I bit my cheek to stop myself from reacting, from crying out at what I saw. Sarah was beside me and we were at the back of a small room. Between us and the door were about half a dozen other women. No, these were not women, but girls. Fuck, every female in this room looked to be around my age. And all of them were at least partially naked. One girl near the side wall was groaning and thrashing her head. A man came over to her and made short work of jabbing a needle into her arm. Once the girl relaxed, he tossed the needle into a bucket before going for his pants. I watched in horror as he pulled his stiff dick out, and lifting one of the girl's legs, he thrust in and began to fuck her. A glance around the room showed three other men fucking equally unresponsive girls. Bile rose up my throat and I closed my eyes against it, focusing on swallowing it down. Someone took my hand and squeezed it. I opened my eyes to see Sarah's scared face. Fuck. We had to be smart to get out of this.

"Pretend to still be high."

I mouthed the words to her and she gave me a nod, before she released my hand. I forced myself to look relaxed. I half closed my eyes and smiled just a little, hoping like hell I looked like I was blissed out. I didn't want them to drug me again. I also fought the urge to pull my shirt closed. It had been ripped up the center and my bra had been opened. It had a front clasp so I hoped it was just open and not broken. If we did get out of here, it would be nice to not have to walk home with my boobs out. Thankfully my pants were on and intact. I just needed to suck it up and accept that for the moment, my boobs were on display. Whenever one of the men glanced our way, we'd hum and grin a little wider. Relief washed over me when they made comments about us being lightweights and that they'd deal with us later.

We kept our act up, eventually feigning sleep as we listened to the endless rapes that went on around us. There were two other girls at the back of the room with us. When they'd each woken, they'd cried out for help. The help they got was another dose of drugs and more of their clothing removed. Part of me couldn't believe they were falling for my and Sarah's act but I guess with so many girls in the room, they either didn't care or weren't keeping track of which girls had been drugged when. From what I could tell, the men delivered the drugs on an as-needed basis. No one was writing anything down or looking at watches.

Eventually the room grew quiet, and the lights were turned off, save one small lamp in the corner. Well, it was quiet of male voices. The other girls still moaned and groaned... and threw up. But after a while it became clear we'd been left to our own devices for the night—or morning. I had no idea what time it was and this room had no windows. Locking my gaze with Sarah's, I reached for my bra and fastened it back up before I took hold of her hand and gave it a squeeze.

"We need to get out of here. Are you able to move?"

I wasn't sure what they'd given us, I guessed heroin. I'd never had it before so wasn't sure what to expect as far as what happens when you come down off it. I felt a little foggy in my head, but physically I seemed okay. I wouldn't know for sure until I tried to stand up, but I knew better than to even try that while there were still bikers in the room.

"Yep, arms and legs all move. Let's get out of here. Do we try to take the others with us?"

I shook my head. "I wish we could, but they're all too drugged up. We'd just end up all getting caught. No, it's better if just us two escape. We can let the cops know what's going on and they can come save the others."

In the dim light I saw Sarah nod and take a deep breath. Still holding hands, we rose slowly from our mattresses and began to move around the other girls. I tried to not look at them, their faces and bodies. The smell was bad enough. I knew if we did manage to make it out of this hell-hole, I was going to be having nightmares for a very long time.

By the time we made it to the closed door, my stomach was churning and bile was rising up my throat. I couldn't hold it back. Thankfully, there were several buckets around the room for just that purpose so I leaned over and retched into one of them. I felt like shit. I leaned against the wall for a moment and Sarah rubbed a hand over my back.

"We need to keep moving. We can't get caught."

She didn't need to say that someone might have heard me retching and be on their way to drug me. I gave her a nod and forced myself to get moving. Taking the lead, I slowly opened the door and peeked out. The hallway looked clear and the whole place seemed quiet. We both slipped out and Sarah shut the door, cutting off the moans and groans. The silence was almost spooky, but neither of us stopped to think about it. On light feet, we dashed toward the front of the building. We passed several sleeping men and a few women on our way, but no one stirred awake to catch us as we made our way out the front door and away.

Without releasing my hold on Sarah's hand, I patted my pockets. The cash I'd stuffed in my back pocket was still there, and my house keys were in the front pocket. Maybe we'd get lucky and find a cab.

Twenty minutes later, because the clubhouse was way out of town, we finally made it home. Unlocking the front door of the dark house, I slipped through first, tugging Sarah along with me.

"And where in the hell have you two been?"

I froze on the spot. Dammit, our foster father had stayed up waiting for us. I couldn't think of a lie that would get us out of trouble, and clearly neither could Sarah as she began stammering about what had happened. It took her a good ten minutes to get her story out as she stood behind me, pressed up against my back. I tried to see our foster father's face, to gauge his reaction, but the room was too dim. When Sarah finished, the room fell into silence.

I held my breath, unsure what his reaction would be. I'd had been living here since I was a toddler. Sarah had come to live here when she was ten. Ron and Sue had always taken care of us, and when we aged out of the system, they didn't boot us to the curb like many foster families did to their kids. However, we'd seriously pushed our luck tonight. Which is something neither of us had ever done before, so I had no idea what his reaction would be.

Slowly he moved toward the wall where he flipped the light switch on. Then he ran his gaze over us.

"You should have told me your plans. I could have told you what would have happened, could have warned you. Are you sure no one saw you leave?"

Sarah buried her face against my back. She was shorter than me, so I felt her tears wet the back of my shirt.

"I'm sure. They would have stopped us if they'd seen us outside. We were on foot, it wouldn't have been hard for them to pick us up." I paused to clear my throat. "We got lucky."

"Damn straight you did." He paused to rub his hands over his face. "This isn't good, girls. The Iron Hammers won't just let you two go. If they see you in the street, they'll grab you. If you try to go to the cops about the other girls, you'll end up back there. You're both young, you don't understand how this town works yet. But the Iron Hammers *own* this town. We tried to shelter you two from it, thought we were doing the right thing. Guess not. I should have told you what they do, how they have cops in their pocket. The way runaway girls disappear."

The longer Ron spoke, the more lightheaded I felt. I still had Sarah's hand in mine and I clung tightly to her. We were so screwed.

"What can we do? I don't want to ever go back to that place. Be used like those other girls are."

With a shake of his head, Ron came over to us and pulled us to him for a hug.

"Ah, my dear girls, there is only one place you can go I'm afraid. And we can't wait. You both need to go shower, change and pack your bags. I'll get the car ready to take you."

"Where?"

I needed to know where we were going, even though I knew I wouldn't know where it was. I'd never left the Galveston area my whole life. Never needed, or wanted, to.

"Bridgewater. It's about an hour northeast from here. The Charon MC runs that town and they are the only ones that can keep you two safe. I've met a couple of them in my travels before. Good men, a little rough around the edges, but they're good men. They won't do to you what the Hammers will."

My tears started to flow as I led Sarah back to our rooms. How the hell had a simple night out ended in such turmoil? For the sake of a little rebellious fun, we'd both just lost everything.

Except each other. We'd always have each other. We might not be blood sisters, but over the past eight years, we'd bonded as though we were.

Scout

While it wasn't unheard of to have someone knocking at my door at five in the morning, it wasn't exactly the norm. So on my way to answer it, I grabbed my gun and checked it as I walked. A peek through the keyhole had me lowering the weapon and opening the door.

"Hey, Ron, what's going on?"

Ron was a bank manager working down in Galveston now, but he'd been at the bank here in Bridgewater for years before he transferred down there. He'd always taken good care of me, as he had my folks before they'd moved to Florida when they'd retired. If I recalled correctly, he used to commute up from Galveston each day so it had made sense when he took a job closer to home. None of that helped clue me in as to why the fuck he was standing on my porch with two girls looking scared out of their minds at five in the fucking morning, though.

"Can we come in? I need your help."

With a nod, I moved to allow the three of them to enter my home. I was still getting used to this big old house being mine. I'd come home after leaving the USMC last year and my folks had promptly told me now I was back, I could take over the shop and they were retiring down to Florida. Suddenly, I'd found myself with a bike shop to run and a big old house to take care of. So far it was working out all right, except for this house that felt so empty with just me rattling around in it. It was also handy that I liked bikes, liked them so much I was part of the local motorcycle club, the Charon MC. I'd prospected in when I'd turned eighteen, and now nine years later, which had included my four year stint in the USMC, I was an enforcer for the club and was working my way to hopefully one day becoming president.

Flicking on the safety, I tucked my gun into the back of my pants as I led my unexpected guests into the kitchen where Ron ushered the girls to sit at my table before he stood behind them. The pair sure were pretty. One blonde, one brunette. The blonde seemed rather subdued, as though life had kicked the shit out of her and she wasn't sure if it was worth the effort to keep going. The brunette on the other hand, she was a fighter and had caught my attention from the moment I'd looked into her eyes when she'd walked into my house. Her chin was up and she had her jaw clenched. I could tell from her eyes that she'd been crying recently, but her gaze had a glint to it that said she was not going to lie down and take whatever the fuck it was that had just landed in her lap.

"So, Ron, care to tell me what has you in my home at five in the morning with two pretty girls in tow?"

"These are my foster daughters, Sarah" he nodded to the blonde, "and Marie." He nodded at the brunette. "And they screwed up last night. Bad."

I ran my gaze over the pair again. I doubted either of them were over twenty-one. "They don't look old enough to have fucked up enough that you need my help. What happened?"

"The Iron Hammers."

I groaned at those three words. The Iron Hammers MC were a bastard of a club that ran out of Galveston, and they were the type of club that gave MCs a shitty rep. I could only imagine what the girls had been through with them. I focused on the two, zeroing in on the brunette, Marie.

"What'd you do?"

"Ah, we got invited out to a party at their clubhouse. Soon after we arrived, we got cornered. Um, they held us down to drug us up." She cleared her throat. "We managed to escape later, after they'd all passed out. Dad says we can't stay in town now, that they'll come for us if we do."

I wasn't fucking born yesterday. I knew there was a whole lot more to that story than what she was telling me. But they both looked like they'd been through enough already and Ron was right. They couldn't stay in Galveston, the Hammers would find them.

"He's right. It's no longer safe for you to be anywhere near the Iron Hammers. Good news is your pops here knew where it would be safe for you. Those fuckers won't step foot in Bridgewater. You'll be safe here. And you can live here with me until you find your feet. My folks moved out and left me this huge fucking house to live in. If the pair of you help me keep it clean and tidy, maybe cook a meal or two for me, we'll call it even. Two things I need to know— do the Hammers know your names and do either of you have jobs?"

"We didn't have ID with us, and they never asked our names. And I'm a waitress at a small family-owned diner in the center of town and Sarah's a cashier at Kroger."

At least they wouldn't need new IDs. That made things simpler. I ran a palm over my head, trying to think of work options.

"I'm not sure what we can offer you for work. I'll have a chat with my prez in a couple hours and see what we can come up with to fit your skills."

Ron moved from where he stood behind the girls toward me.

"Thank you for this, and you let me know if they need anything at all."

I took the business card he held out. I could see in his expression this was breaking his heart. These girls might be foster and not his by blood, but he clearly loved them and to have to send them away like this was tearing him up.

"I promise I'll take good care of them for you. You did the right thing getting them out of Galveston immediately."

He nodded, then cleared his throat. "They've got a few bags in the car. I'll just go grab them, then I need to head back to Sue. She's a mess over all this."

"I'll come give you a hand. Girls? Stay in the house."

I doubted the Iron Hammers had followed their vehicle, but it was always better to be safe than sorry. That, and I wouldn't mind a couple minutes alone with Ron. As I closed the door behind me and followed him to his car, I spoke up.

"You and Sue are welcome to come visit whenever you like. It's not safe for the girls to go back to Galveston, but considering the Hammers don't know who the girls are, you and Sue should be safe enough to come and visit."

He nodded absently as he opened the trunk and leaned in to grab one of the bags inside.

"They're good girls. Both of them. They've never caused us any trouble."

"Until now."

He chuffed a laugh as he handed me a suitcase.

"Yeah. Until now."

A thought occurred to me. Neither had mentioned school when I'd asked about employment, but just because they weren't at school didn't mean they were over eighteen.

"How old are they? Are they're adults? I don't want to get accused of kidnapping or some shit with this."

"Yes, they're legally adults. Both have had their eighteenth birthdays in the last six months. You won't get in any trouble with the authorities for having them in your home."

That was a relief. I was more than happy to help out Ron with this shit, but it was a fucking relief I could do it legally.

After we both loaded up with their bags, we headed back inside. I called out as we passed the kitchen.

"C'mon, girls. I'll show you your new rooms."

Thankfully, my folks had left a lot of their furniture behind so the spare bedrooms had beds and wardrobes in them. The girls and Ron followed me as I led the way toward the back of the house. The two guest rooms were separated by a bathroom, and I showed them all three rooms.

"Pick whichever room you like. Take your time getting settled in and maybe try to catch some shuteye. You've had a shit night by the sounds of things. I need to head over to the shop in a couple of hours, but I'll drop back for lunch and we'll chat some more then about what's gonna happen from here on out. Okay?"

They both nodded, but before they could even enter a room, Ron spoke up that he needed to head off, so we all followed him to the front of the house. Both Sarah and Marie were crying when they hugged the man. I shook his hand then he was gone. And I had two new housemates. Including one that had my cock twitching for her. *Fuck.*

"Will we have a say in what we're gonna do for work?"

Marie had wiped the tears from her face and was glaring at me like I was going to suggest she eat nails or something.

"You're both adults and are free to live however you like. However, Ron was right when he said that you can't stay in Galveston. Unless you *want* to end up with the Hammers?"

I cocked a brow as the color drained from both their faces.

"Yeah, didn't think so. The only reason I'm suggesting I ask my prez about work is to make your move here easier. If you gotta go through interviews and shit, without references, it could take you a long fucking time to find something. Ron brought you here so I could keep you protected and take care of you both. Let me do what I just promised I would."

"Thank you."

They both whispered the words at the same time.

"You're welcome. We've all made shitty choices in life. I'm just glad you both got out of that shit hole in one piece. Now, go on back and pick a room and settle in for a nap. I'm gonna go get ready for work and head out. I'll bring some food back with me for lunch so you don't need to worry about making anything."

I stayed standing in my hallway, hands on my hips as I watched them walk back to their rooms. My gaze lowered to Marie's ass as it swayed with her movements, and my cock hardened and throbbed for some attention. With a shake of my head I made my way to my own room. She was nine fucking years younger than me. And about as innocent as you could get. No way would she ever want some fucked up veteran like me. I needed to keep my hands off, and hopefully before too long both girls would have jobs and move out into their own places. Remove the temptation so I wouldn't cave and go after what I shouldn't want.

Chapter 1

29th November 2017
Marie

Was this man for real?

"You can't be serious!"

Over the twenty-five years since I'd first met Scout, he'd never before asked me to do something like this. Did he truly not understand how I felt about him? How much it was going to hurt me to see this girl who'd had the one thing I desperately wanted, probably many times, every day in my shop?

"C'mon, Marie. I don't understand the problem. With Zara only working part time, you need more reliable staff. I can guarantee Missy, I mean Mercedes, will be. Now that Tiny's claimed her as his old lady, she won't up and leave you like all those teenagers do. And she won't need much training, she used to work in the kitchen back at that commune she was raised in."

With a growl, I spun away from the infuriating man and started to pace the length of my small living room. He knew I was a sucker for a sob story, and Mercedes sure as hell had one. I'd heard the tale from Zara. Her mother had fled from Mexico with her when she was a toddler, and they'd gotten caught up with a cult-like commune. She'd run from the place after she'd found her mother murdered and had landed on the Charon MC's doorstep—where she became one of their whores. One of the lucky women who got to touch and be touched by Scout, the president of the Charon MC and the man who'd held my heart for over twenty years.

I rubbed over the ache in my chest. You'd think after all this time I would have gotten over my crush on this man. I wasn't a young woman anymore, the hero worship I'd suffered with when I'd first came to Bridgewater was long past. Maybe his asking this of me would be enough to get my stupid heart to cut the shit and move on. Because for him to ask, with no clue how much it would hurt, made it clear he didn't give a damn about me. At least not like that.

Frustrated, I turned back to face him. Even all these years later he was a good looking man. His hair and beard had more gray than dark brown these days, the lines around his eyes more pronounced, but he still made my ovaries sigh. Even with that stupid bandana he insisted on wearing all the damn time.

"When was the last time you fucked her?"

He jerked back, his eyes widening. Yeah, I didn't curse often anymore, but what else could I call what he did with all those young women? He sure as hell didn't make love to them. At least I hoped like hell he didn't.

"Ah, I'm not sure. Six months, maybe. She's not a club whore anymore. She and Tiny are exclusive. Why are you getting so worked up over this?"

It was my turn to look shocked. Was he really that clueless?

"Why, indeed." I shook my head and took a deep breath. "Fine, whatever. Get her to come around tomorrow and I'll give her a trial run, see how she goes. I can't promise more than that."

"Thanks, babe."

A smile stretched his mouth and his body relaxed, which just pissed me off even more.

"Now you've got what you came for, get out of my house. And you don't need to come with her tomorrow. I promise I won't bite her or anything."

His face returned to an expression of confusion and shock, but I was so far past caring about his feelings. Walking by him, I opened my front door and waited for him to get the hint and get the hell out of my house.

"Marie? What the fuck is wrong?"

Glaring at him, I tried to formulate words to express what he just asked of me but couldn't come up with anything that would say what I wanted to.

"Scout, the fact you need me to explain is exactly why I'm not going to. Get out of my hair already. I've got pies to bake."

With a frown, he slowly made his way toward me, and when he reached a palm out, I tensed and glared harder at him until he dropped his hand and slunk out the door.

The second he passed through it, I had it shut and bolted. Then I slid to the floor and let the tears fall as silent sobs shook my body.

I was turning forty-three years old on Sunday, dammit. Way too old to be crushing on a man who didn't want me. Somehow the years had all passed me by. Now I was getting older and still all alone. No husband, no kids. No grandkids. Zara was such a sweetheart, she'd told me I was her little daughter Cleo's adoptive gramma. Looking down at my stomach, I spread my fingers over the area. What would it have felt like to have a life growing within me? My cycles were still regular, so technically it wasn't too late yet. *At least in theory.* But if I kept waiting around for Scout, it surely would be before he woke up and smelled the roses.

Taking another deep breath, I wiped my tears away and rose from the floor to head to the bathroom. After splashing some cold water over my face and drying off, I headed to my kitchen. I'd pour all my stress and worry into making some extra pies for the shop. For as long as I could remember, I'd always found solace in baking so I prayed it helped me today.

The longer I spent whipping and mixing, the calmer I felt about my newest employee. I hadn't met Mercedes before, but from how Zara spoke about her, she was nervous around the other old ladies, and didn't really know how to act out in the world. My heart gave a jolt for a different reason. Wondering how old she was, I pondered how to best help her. If she wasn't used to dealing with strangers, she may not do well on the counter where she had to take orders, but hopefully she'd be fine with delivering orders to start with. There were often several of the Charon men in the cafe so that should help her feel more at ease.

However, if I found out she wasn't exclusively with Tiny, that she was still having sex with whoever caught her eye, she'd be out so fast she wouldn't see the door before it hit her on the ass.

Scout

After leaving Marie's house, I headed back to the clubhouse. I had no fucking clue why she was so damn upset with me. I thought she'd like being able to help out a girl like Mercedes. She really was a sweet kid, and much better suited to waitressing than whoring. Not that she wasn't good at it. Nope, that girl had some serious skills. Tiny was a lucky fucker to have her all to himself. But she had a sweet nature that deserved more out of life than that of a whore. She deserved a man of her own, a family to take care of, and a job she could be proud of.

Marie did too. But she'd never settled down with anyone. Come to think of it, I couldn't recall her even dating over the years. That had me frowning. Surely she hadn't stayed single for the last, what, twenty five or so years since she'd come to town. I frowned and adjusted my bandana. Why the fuck had she stayed single? Surely it wasn't because...

"What's got you looking so worried?"

I dropped my hands down to the desk as Bulldog, my best friend and VP, came in, shut the door and made himself comfortable on the couch.

"So many things, brother. Would you like a list?"

Bulldog chuckled. "It's been like that lately, hasn't it?"

"Just a touch. Just hung up with Viper. They're gonna up the use of the bunker."

Viper was the president of the Satan's Cowboys MC. One of the biggest MCs in Texas, they were firmly above the Charon MC on the food chain and we needed to make sure they were happy with us. That included helping them run their shit through our fucking town. I didn't like it. Not one bit. But they'd found out about the old bunker out on the gun range that some doomsdayer had built way back when, and wanted it as a layover for their weapons and drug runs. The Charons had always kept Bridgewater drug free, and I'd made sure Viper understood that just because they were running their shit through our town, I didn't want to see any of it stopping to stay here. Thankfully, he'd agreed. But it still pissed me off to have so much illegal shit happening so close to us, and us helping out with it. For the most part, the Charons were legit. We earned our money through the bar, gym and bike shop. Sure, we did the odd weapons run for the Cowboys and earned our piece from that. But until last April, it had been once or twice a year. Now it was going to be more than once a fucking month and that shit made me nervous.

"Ah, fuck. Not sure that's a good move. They start putting too much shit through there, people are gonna start to notice. Once that happens, it won't take long before the authorities are sniffing around out there."

"I know, brother. And I told Viper that. Not that it fucking matters. They'll do what they want."

He nodded. "You been to see Marie yet?"

"Yeah, she's gonna give Mercedes a go. But she's not happy about it for some fucking reason."

That made him laugh. He tried to cover it with a cough, but I knew the bastard.

"What's so fucking funny?"

"You being so fucking clueless. It's hilarious."

With a huff, I got up and grabbed the bottle of whiskey I kept over on a shelf and two glasses. Not that Bulldog deserved a drink after that comment. As I poured, I raised my eyebrow at him, silently asking him to settle the fuck down and explain.

"Oh, man. Seriously? You don't get it?"

"You sound like Marie. What do I not get, that everyone else fucking does?"

"That woman has had her heart set on your stupid ass since the moment she came into town. And you've just asked her to take care of a girl she knows you've fucked. Marie might not be officially part of the club, but she'd hear enough talk at the cafe, especially with Zara working down there, to know that Mercedes was a club whore. Do I need to keep explaining this shit to you? We all figured you were into her too, just being a stubborn jackass for some fucked-up reason. But maybe we've all had it wrong all this time. Do you really not care for her at all? Because I've seen how your eyes follow her around. Don't even think of fucking lying to me."

The way Bulldog talked, it sounded like the whole fucking club had been speculating. Were they seriously all that fucking bored?

"Don't be stupid. She just had some hero worship thing going on when she first came to town. She got over that."

Or rather, I'd broken her of that. I could still remember clearly the six weeks she'd lived under my roof. Could remember that final day when I'd woken up to find her beneath me in my bed. With my fucking hand wrapped around her throat. I'd had another fucking nightmare and Marie, with her big heart, had tried to wake me from it, and not realizing it was her, I'd tried to kill her. Two days later she moved out.

"Even you have to realize how fucking wrong you are on that score. And what about you? How do *you* feel about her? Because, brother, you've left that woman—a good woman—on the shelf for over twenty years. She's not gonna stay there forever, especially if you pull shit like asking her to employ one of your past lays."

"She's nine fucking years younger than me. I'm too old for her."

I threw back my whiskey before I poured another one.

"Still not hearing the answer I'm looking for."

Huffing out a breath I looked up and locked my gaze with Bulldog. Bulldog, who was happily married. Bulldog, who'd gotten his shit together young and now had a family, an old lady, a niece/surrogate daughter, and now a grandson.

"I've wanted her from the first instant I saw her. That's never changed. But the other thing that's also never changed? I'm not good enough for her. I'm too fucked up to settle down."

Bulldog shook his head as a look of sadness filled his gaze.

"First, that nine years might have made a difference when she was eighteen, but the woman's over forty now. Nine years is fucking nothing, and you know it. And you're one of the best men I know. The nightmares and shit you had back then have settled down these days, right?"

I nodded. After I'd woken up with my fingers wrapped around Marie's throat, I'd sucked it up and gone to the head doc. Went through all the counseling and came out on the other side being able to fucking sleep. I still had the odd dream, but nothing compared to what I'd been suffering before I'd gone to get help.

"It would still be dangerous for her to be associated with me. Being president comes with risks. I care for her enough, I don't want to see her fucking hurt."

"Seriously? The entire club, and most of the town, has considered that woman your old lady for years. You eat more often in her cafe than you do at home, she comes to the clubhouse for the family parties. She's currently in as much danger as she would be if you claimed her ass. I know there's been several men over the years attempt to make a move on her that one of our brothers has dealt with."

That had me jerking in my seat. "You telling me she's been single all this time because our brothers have made sure it was that way? Fuck, man. How does she not hate me?"

"No fucking clue, brother. Not many women would have hung around this long. Do us all a favor and man the fuck up, Scout, and go get your woman. Haven't you both waited long enough already?"

Unable to think of an answer, I lifted my glass to suck back my drink. Lost in my head, I barely noticed Bulldog leave, closing the door behind himself. Had she really been waiting on me all these years? Because, I'd never admit it out loud, but every one of the club whores I fucked, I imagined it was her I was doing. Ever since the first day when Ron woke me up at five in the fucking morning to deliver his foster daughters into my care. Fuck. I'd done such a great job of that, hadn't I? I had no fucking clue where Sarah was anymore. Hadn't for years now. She'd not stayed living in my house long. Less than a month before she'd found her own place. She'd made it clear that bikers scared her and she wanted nothing to do with any of us. When I'd made it clear to her she was free to leave but that she couldn't ever return to Galveston so long as the Iron Hammers ruled down there, she'd told me not to worry, she'd never go south again. When I'd passed that on to Ron, he'd told me to leave her be. That he'd expected her to take off. In fact, he'd been waiting for her to do just that for months before they went to the party that turned their lives upside down.

And look where Marie was, thanks to me. Sure, I'd helped her get work, then helped again when she wanted to set up her own cafe. Of course I helped her move out after I nearly killed her. And then what? She'd pined after me for the next twenty five years? While every time some man showed any interest in her, my boys ran them off. How the fuck could I have not noticed that had been going on? I should have been firmer with her back at the start, and with the club.

She could do better.

She deserved better.

Fuck. It would kill me to watch her with another man. I winced and filled my glass again. I was such an asshole. If the mere thought of her with another man had me wanting to go shoot someone, how the fuck had she felt over the years knowing I was here fucking all the wet and willing that paraded through this place?

Bulldog was wrong. I wasn't a good man. Fuck, I'd been doing one hell of a number on the only woman, aside from my mother, who'd ever mattered to me. That made me a first rate bastard, nothing more.

Chapter 2

Marie

"Ah, Marie? Are you doing okay?"

I stopped for a moment from settling the fourth pie into the display fridge to turn to Zara.

"I'm just fine, sugar. Why'd you ask?"

She looked from me to the pies, then back to my face. "We don't normally have that many different options, especially this late in the week. And I've been working for you long enough to know what that level of baking means. Did Scout pull some stupid stunt again?"

My cheeks heated. Dammit. Was I that transparent? *Probably best to just gloss right over that question of hers.*

"So, we've got a new girl coming in today."

Zara stiffened and her shoulders rose. "Are you replacing me? Because if you need me to work more days, I can. Cleo's settling nicely into a routine now, and Mac can get some of the others to help out at the gym so he can watch her more often."

Placing the cake in its place I turned back toward Zara with both palms up to stop her. With her cataplexy, she'd give herself an attack if she got any more worked up. "Whoa. I'd never replace you. Not ever. Scout's asked me to take on Mercedes. I thought it might be nice to have another person trained up. Means each of us can take a little time off here and there, right?"

She put a palm to her chest as she chuckled. "Way to scare the shit outta me, Marie. Damn. Guess that explains the pies too, huh? Are you really okay having Mercedes here? I mean, you know, considering what she was..."

Stupid tears pricked my eyes, but I refused to let even one fall.

"It's not her fault Scout's a manwhore. It was his choice to go to her." *Not me.* I silently added.

Zara came over to me and wrapped her arms around me and hugged me to her for a few moments.

"I've met her once or twice. She's always been really sweet to everyone. And Tiny certainly seems happier now she's back and with him. And if it makes you feel better, once Tiny took a shine to her—which was pretty much as soon as he saw her—the others all left her alone, so I doubt Scout was with her often."

"Sugar, you know I love you as though you were my daughter, right?"

She nodded.

"You need to just leave this alone. Scout and me, well, we're what we'll always be and there's nothing that's gonna change things."

And wasn't that the truth. Nothing I'd done over the years had gotten me that man's attention. It was time I stepped away from him and the club. Well, as much as I could with the way they all came in here on the regular, anyhow. It was in moments like this that I missed Sarah. She would have dragged me out years ago to maybe Houston or Dallas, where we would be able to meet men who weren't so scared of Scout and the Charons that they wouldn't even talk to us. Maybe I should go away by myself. Zara could open and close for me, and if Mercedes proved useful, they'd easily be able to handle a Saturday on their own. I could head up to Houston for a weekend away. Go out, maybe meet a man, have some fun. Get laid. Hell, it had been so long I wondered if my body had forgotten what it even was. At least, when it didn't involve a vibrator. The few men I'd tried to go out with over the years had run for the hills as soon as they learned I was tangled up with the Charons. I was pretty sure one of the boys had words with each of the men and made them run off, but I couldn't prove it. If I'd been able to work out who'd spoken up, I'd have had some pretty nasty words of my own to say to them.

"Um, Marie? Whatcha plotting?"

"Nothing much. Just thinking a weekend up in Houston to celebrate my birthday next Sunday might be nice. Think you can handle the place Saturday?"

Her eyes widened, like I'd shocked her. *Probably had.* Anyone that knew me, knew I didn't ever leave town for anything.

"Of course I can. But I didn't realize it was your birthday! We should throw you a party at the clubhouse."

I shook my head. "No, that's not necessary at all. I don't need some party. But a nice, relaxing weekend away might be good. No biker chaperones either, missy."

I gave Zara a firm look, knowing full well the woman would tell her man, Mac, who'd tell Scout, who'd put freaking guards on me and ruin my fun before I could find any.

Zara slowly nodded, and thankfully before she could come up with something to say, the door swung open and a petite girl of Mexican heritage slipped in, looking nervous. Alongside was her huge, muscled, biker body guard, Tiny. Guess this was Mercedes.

"Hey, Marie! Zara. Thanks so much for giving Mercedes this chance."

I'd met Tiny many times before, but I'd never seen him with a woman. He was really sweet with Mercedes. A little clingy for my taste, but clearly it was fine with Mercedes.

"Can always use good workers, Tiny. So, Mercedes, tell me what skills you have that I can use."

I really hoped she wouldn't say anything about what she used to do at the clubhouse. I didn't think I could keep a straight face if she did.

"Ah, um. I worked in the kitchen at the commune. Prep work, serving, cleaning up. Your coffee machine looks way fancier than anything I've ever used before, but I'm a fast learner and a hard worker. I won't make you regret giving me a chance, I promise."

That made me smile. Mercedes might be little and petite, but she was a fighter under the surface. Clearly she knew nothing about whatever the fuck was between me and Scout, which was a relief. We could all just move right along without even touching the subject.

"Sounds like you'll fit in here just fine. Tiny? You heading off so I can get to showing your girl the ropes, or what?"

Over the years, I'd discovered these Charon men needed to be told firmly what they needed to do. If I didn't get rid of him, Tiny would sit in here all day, which would most likely leave Mercedes a nervous mess.

Tiny gave me a smirk before he gave his girl a kiss goodbye and headed out the door.

"You've met Zara before, right?"

She nodded. "Yeah, at the clubhouse."

"Great. Right, well, let's start with a tour, shall we? Then I'll show you how to use that fancy coffee machine."

A broad grin tugged at my lips as I showed the girl around. She and Zara joked and made small talk between customers and by the time the day was over I was confident she'd be a great addition to my little cafe. And that I was going to be able to take my weekend away without a worry about how the cafe would fare without me.

Once I got home, I made quick work of looking up a list of hotels in Houston. When I found a nice, fancy one that had a spa on site, I called and booked myself in. The more I thought about it, a weekend of massages, pampering, no bikers and a night out sounded like heaven. It wasn't like I was hurting for money after working all these years and not doing much with my life. What I needed was to start to live life. Maybe I should book myself in to a hair salon while I was away, get a new look. Maybe go shopping and update my wardrobe. Was a new car too much? I shook my head. Yes, a new car was taking it too far. Zara would accuse me of having a midlife crisis and I'd never hear the end of it.

Feeling positive about my plans, I hummed my way through cooking myself dinner before I sat down to eat it in front of the TV.

It was way past time I started actually living my life.

Scout

After spending the last two days busy working my ass off on a bike rebuild, I was having a few relaxing Friday night beers with Bulldog, Keys and a few of the other brothers at the clubhouse when Mac came rushing in. Sipping my beer I watched him scan the room before his gaze settled on me and stayed there.

"Ah, fuck. Wonder what's happened now?"

Bulldog spoke my thoughts as Mac came barreling over to us and took a seat beside us.

"What the fuck is going on with Marie?"

Bulldog started chuckling and I took another drink, ignoring my VP.

"Nothing. Why?"

"Bullshit, it's nothing. Earlier in the week, dumbass here asked Marie to take on Mercedes as a waitress, without any consideration of how the woman would feel about employing a woman he used to fuck."

Mac winced at Bulldog's explanation before he spoke.

"So you haven't been into her cafe since then?"

I set my bottle down and leaned forward, starting to get worried. "No, figured she could use some space. Why?"

"Well, yesterday was the first time I've ever seen four different types of pie on the menu. Does that seem unusual to you?"

I frowned over at Mac, ignoring the next round of snickering coming from Bulldog. Some best friend he was tonight. "Well, yeah. But as Bulldog's already pointed out, I pissed her off. She bakes to vent. That alone shouldn't have you here all riled up on a Friday night. What the fuck is going on?"

"It's her birthday on Sunday, and to celebrate, she's decided on a weekend away from Bridgewater. Zara's worried about her, told me she didn't seem like her normal self when she spoke about taking tomorrow off and heading out. Marie also told Zara that she didn't want any biker chaperones on her trip."

Ah, fuck. I was terrible with dates, but my phone had reminded me that her birthday was coming up. I'd wondered about surprising her by taking her out for dinner, maybe talk to her about what the fuck was going on between us. The thought of her out in the world on her own, with no protection, didn't sit well with me.

"When's she leavin'? And where is she fucking running off to?"

Mac shook his head. "No clue, prez. Zara only admitted to me that she was going this afternoon because she needs me at home tomorrow to look after Cleo while she runs the cafe for the day."

I pulled out my phone and hit speed dial to call her mobile. When it rang out and went to voicemail, I put away my phone and looked to Keys, our resident tech head. "Find out where the hell my woman is, Keys."

With a nod, he took off toward my office where he kept a laptop.

"She technically ain't yours, Scout. You've got no right to keep her from leaving town."

I glared at Bulldog, my supposed friend. "In the twenty-five years she's been living in town, you know how many times that woman has ventured outside of Bridgewater? Twice. That's it." Despite still being terrified of the Iron Hammers, when each of her foster parents had passed away, she'd gone to the funeral. I'd gone with her to make her feel safer, so I'd seen how the woman was a nervous wreck when she left the safety of our town.

"That was before we cleaned out the Iron Hammers. She's safe now. Even if those bastards who took her were still around, they'd never recognize her now. It's been over twenty years and they only had her for a few hours. There's no active threat to us right now. Relax and let the woman spread her wings a little."

Even though he had some good points, I didn't fucking care.

"She's mine to fucking protect. How exactly am I supposed to do that when I don't even know where the fuck she is?"

Instead of anyone answering me, they all just looked at me with pity in their eyes. I stood with a curse, to head to my office. Hopefully Keys had an answer for me already.

He looked up at me as I stormed into my office, slamming the door behind me.

"Please tell me you know where the fuck she is."

"Not yet. Nearly there, though."

I readjusted my bandana as I paced my office. "How you tracking her down exactly?"

"Her phone right now, then I'll check her car. Remember? I've got GPS trackers on all the girls' phones and vehicles. I don't use them unless I have to, and I sure as hell don't look 'em up for the hell of it. But it helps me sleep at night to know I've got a chance of finding them if some fool decides to take one of them. If you recall, it sure as fuck helped when Zara got snatched."

I shuddered as I remembered what we'd found when we caught up with Zara. Poor woman was barely alive. Fuck, if anything had happened to Marie I'd tear through anyone who had dared touch her.

"Considering we have no reason to assume anything other than Marie is fine and just having a weekend away, what exactly are you planning on doing once we find her?"

I stopped pacing, and after adjusting my bandana again, faced Keys. "I guess I'm gonna go make sure that she's okay. Then watch over her till she comes home."

Keys nodded then sat back from his laptop, staring hard at me.

"What if she's with a man? On a date."

A growl vibrated up my throat before I could call it back. My vision actually turned a little red for a moment at the fury that flowed over me at the thought of her spending the weekend with some other fucker.

"Well, I guess that answers that question. I know you're my president, but you're also my friend. As is Marie, so I'm going to be straight with you on this. If you do not intend on stepping up to fucking claim her, I'm not letting you go check on her. I'll head up there with Arrow, see how she's doing, and go from there. You've had that woman chasing your fucking tail for over twenty years. It's time for you make a fucking decision and quit being so fucking cruel to her."

First Bulldog, now Keys. What the fuck was going on with my brothers lately? Everyone was all up in my fucking personal life and I didn't like it. Especially because they all saw too fucking much.

"Marie's mine. Always has been. Now, fucking tell me where the hell she is so I can go get her back."

He held out his hand. "Give me your phone and I'll program it in for you. That way, if she moves before you can get to her, you'll know where to go. Arrow and I will still ride up with you, just in case something is going on. But if she's just relaxing, we'll leave you to it and head back home."

As I waited for Keys to do his thing with my phone, I began to mentally plan various options for how the weekend would go, depending on what I found when I located Marie.

Chapter 3

Marie

I should have done this years ago! With a wide smile, I made my way back into the hotel with my bulging shopping bags. I now had a whole new wardrobe to take back to Bridgewater with me tomorrow. I'd driven up last night, but didn't go out. Instead I'd had a long soak in the spa bath in my room before lying in bed and watching a romantic comedy. Then I fell into a nice, blissful sleep. Today my mission had been to replace my aged wardrobe. The assistants in the few shops I went to were so lovely, helping me find things that suited by body shape and activity level. Being on my feet all day meant there were some things I just couldn't wear all day long. Like high heeled shoes. My feet hurt just thinking about it!

This was my second, and last, trip back to the hotel to drop off bags. I was due at the salon in twenty minutes to have my hair and nails done. Then, tonight I was going out. I didn't care I was on my own, I was going to go have a few drinks at the bar. Hopefully I'd meet someone to dine with—if not, well, I didn't care. I was going to go eat fancy food, and drink over-priced drinks. No matter what happened this weekend, I vowed to myself that I would have fun doing it. So far, that had held true. After fifteen years of owning my own business and not ever spending much money, I had more than enough in my savings to splash out all I wanted without worry. Which I was grateful for, because this weekend away was exactly what I'd needed. In the last twenty-four hours I'd only heard a couple of Harleys, but I'd not seen them or their riders, so I didn't care. I was free!

It was a few hours later that I started to feel less than joyous. I'd chickened out at the salon and not gone with a new style. Instead, I just got a trim and blow dry. The nail technician who took care of my nails was an expert. I didn't get fake nails, but got a full manicure and pedicure before this absolute artist painted and drew all over my nails. The little swirls and dabs of glitter that caught the light had me smiling again. Even if it was only for a little while.

Now I was sitting in the bar area feeling down as I sipped my drink and scanned the room. This part of my plan wasn't going so well. The bar here at the hotel was filled with tired looking businessmen or couples. With a sigh, I lifted my drink to take yet another sip. An image of Scout filled my mind and I let my mind wander, imagining what it would be like if he were here with me. Would he have dutifully walked around with me today? Carrying my bags and telling me how pretty I looked in each new outfit? The thought of him in all his biker gear, weighed down with my shopping bags had me chuckling. Maybe I shouldn't have taken off like I had without telling anyone exactly where I was. I knew Zara was worried about me, and figured she'd tattled on me when I got the call from Scout last night. The call I'd not answered. I winced. That was gonna come back and bite me in the ass, I was sure. Scout wasn't a man who liked to be ignored.

When my drink was finished I twirled the straw for a minute as I tried to decide if I really wanted another one. And if I really wanted to sit in a restaurant with all these happy couples to eat alone. Maybe it would be best if I just went up to my room and ordered room service. Tomorrow I could go enjoy my massage then head back home and get on with life. *Apparently forever alone.* My eyes stung at the thought, that I'd left it too late to meet someone special.

"Hey, pretty lady."

Oh hell, that voice. I knew that voice. How had he found me? Surely he hadn't followed me. Taking a deep breath, I blinked back the moisture in my eyes before I looked up. All the questions I wanted to ask vanished from my mind as I took in how different he looked. Gone were all the things that identified him as the president of the Charon MC. I silently blinked up at him as he set a fresh drink in front of me. He was wearing a white button up shirt with black jeans, the large Harley Davidson belt buckle the only sign of his love of bikes. The bandana was missing from his head, and it looked like he'd had his hair and beard trimmed recently. When he leaned down to brush a kiss over my cheek, my brain started firing again. Ignoring how good his soft beard felt against my skin, I frowned at him as he sat opposite me at the high table I'd been at for the past half hour or so.

"What are you doing here, Scout?"

He smiled like he had every right to be sitting with me here. "I thought we could have dinner together, an early birthday celebration."

I didn't say a word, but raised an eyebrow at him. He knew full well that wasn't enough of an answer.

After a few moments, he started squirming in his seat a little. He raised his hand to his head, no doubt looking to adjust his bandana like he did so often, but he wasn't wearing one, so he dropped his hand back onto the table with a small huff.

"What the fuck did you think I was gonna do when you took off without letting anyone know where you were going?"

"You do realize I'm an adult, right? I can do whatever I like, with whoever I like, whenever I like. I told Zara I was going to Houston for the weekend when I asked her to run the cafe for me while I was gone. I fail to see who else I needed to inform."

I did my best not to chuckle when he got all flustered, but the man was adorable all dressed up and going a little red in the face.

"Marie, you need to tell *me*. You know? The one who promised to keep you safe? The one who worries every fucking day that someone is gonna come take you from me!"

That had me jerking back in my seat in surprise. Was that the reason why he was always hovering around me but never showing any indication he wanted to take things further? He was simply honoring his promise to a dead man? "You made that promise to a man who's now gone. And I'm no longer that vulnerable young woman. The Iron Hammers are no longer a threat to me."

My stupid eyes started stinging again. I didn't know what to think. My heart ached and my head was starting to pound. Before he could respond, I spoke again.

"Just stop with the bullshit, Scout. I can't take it anymore. Just be straight with me for once and tell me what you want from me."

My voice was rough with emotion and the moisture in my eyes was building up and making my sight blurry. I was about two seconds from dashing away to lock myself in my room when he reached over and wrapped his hand around my wrist. Holding my breath, I lifted my gaze until it locked with his. He tugged at my arm until I rose to stand, then he pulled me in toward him until I was standing between his muscular thighs. Still holding my gaze, he dropped my wrist and cupped my face between his palms.

"I want you. I came here tonight to claim what I should have claimed decades ago."

Before I could do more than gasp, his lips were on mine and he was kissing me. My eyes slid shut as sparks buzzed through my blood and butterflies took flight in my stomach. His lips were soft and his beard tickled my skin as he took my mouth with his. I lifted my hands to his chest, stroking his hard pecs through the thin material of his shirt.

When he finally broke the kiss, I tried to chase his mouth for more. I could kiss this man forever and be happy. He held my face firm and rested his forehead against mine.

"No more games, sweetheart. I've been a fool, but that's over. You're mine, Marie. Always have been, always will be. Now, how about we start off our night right and go get some dinner?"

I was tempted to pinch myself to check I was awake.

"And will I get a goodnight kiss at the end of this night?"

"Oh, babe, I'm hoping to give you a whole lot more lovin' than just a kiss by the end of the night."

My temperature shot through the roof as my imagination took his words and ran with them. Suddenly, my night was looking up. Guess coming to Houston to find a date wasn't such a bad idea after all, even if the date had followed me from back home.

Scout

By the time I handed over my credit card to the waiter at the end of our dinner, I was more in love with Marie than I'd been before. I'd stayed in the shadows for most of the day, watching her go from shop to shop. Seeing her so fucking happy had made me crave to be a part of her happiness. So, as I trailed behind her, I visited a few shops of my own, picking up a nice shirt and new jeans for tonight, along with getting my hair and beard trimmed. Hell, I even took off my bandana. I couldn't remember the last time I'd done that. It was pretty damn rare for me to be without my Charon cut, too. But for Marie, to give her this illusion of a biker-free weekend, I'd done it without a second thought. Then, just now as we'd eaten our fill, we'd chatted about anything and everything. But she hadn't asked about how I'd found her yet, which surprised me. I kinda figured that would have been her first question.

"Ah, so did you just ride up today or do you have a room here?"

"I rode up last night, so yeah, I have a room here."

Not sure how she'd take the news I had a room on the same floor as her. Keys was a great hacker when he put his mind to it, so I had the information I'd needed to request a room on the same floor as her. It was probably best I didn't share with her how that happened, though.

The expression that crossed her face left me frowning. I wasn't sure if she was pissed at me, or just deep in thought. It didn't take long for her to speak up.

"Are you trying to tell me that you spent most of your day today following me around town?"

Still unsure if she was angry with me over it, I shrugged in response. "I grabbed myself a few things while I was out, but yeah. Needed to make sure you were safe."

"How did you find where I was in the first place?"

I gave her a smirk. No way was I throwing Keys under that bus. "I have my ways."

She glared at me a minute before the expression faded. "My phone. Like you had Keys do to save Zara."

She was right, but I wasn't confirming it. Thankfully the waiter returning with my card and the receipt for me to sign saved me from having to come up with something. Once that was all done, I stood and held my hand out to Marie. She put her palm in mine and I pulled her in against me so I could give her another short kiss.

"What do you want to do now, love?"

A cheeky smile spread over her lips as she looked up at me through her lashes. "We could go up to my room for a night cap."

I stared at her for a moment, trying to gauge if she was suggesting what I fucking hoped she was. I cupped her face with one palm, tilting her head up so she was looking directly into my eyes.

"No more games, Marie. We go to your room, I'm gonna take you. Understand?"

Her pupils dilated as she melted against me a little. I hoped like fuck I wasn't currently dreaming.

"No more games. Take me, make me yours."

After giving her another fast, hard kiss, I took her hand and strode off to the elevators. I was tempted to sling her over my shoulder and run, so we could get there faster, but I didn't think she'd like that. Especially when I was trying to be civilized for her tonight. Once in the elevator, I raised my hand to hit the button for the fourth floor but stopped before I hit it. I wasn't supposed to know what floor.

"What floor, babe?"

"Four."

After I hit the button, I wrapped my arm around her waist and hauled her in against me. I fucking loved how she felt pressed up to me. How much better would it feel when we were both naked? A shiver ran down my spine. I could hardly believe that after waiting twenty-five fucking years, I was finally going to have this woman beneath me.

When we stopped, I let her take the lead so I got to watch her sexy ass sway as she moved down the hall. She'd bought herself new clothes today and the fitted black dress she was wearing looked sexy as hell. I wondered what she was wearing underneath it. Would it be practical or lacy? I licked my lips as I imagined taking it off, no matter what it looked like. My cock was already hard, and it jerked at the thought of having Marie naked and at my mercy. While she dug into her handbag for her room key, I moved up close behind her to wrap my hands around her hips, sliding my palms over the smooth material. Leaning down I nipped her earlobe, and with a whimper she trembled against me. When she finally got the keycard to read, we stumbled into the room together. I put my foot out behind me to kick the door shut while I held her to my front, pressing kisses down her throat she tilted her head and reached a hand back to hold my hip as she shimmied her ass over my groin, making my cock throb for her and a groan rise from my throat.

After lowering the zip on the back of her dress, I pushed the straps of her dress over her shoulders and smoothed my palms down her body until the dress was on the floor at her feet. As I moved back up, I flicked open her bra. She pulled it free from her body while I slipped her panties down her lean legs. I gave her butt cheek a gentle bite as I moved to stand again. I pulled her back flush against me and looked over her shoulder, down her body, seeing her naked for the very first time. I cupped her tits in my palms and her already hard nipples tightened further.

"Fuck, babe. You are fucking gorgeous."

I spun her around and with my body pressed against hers, had her back against the wall and a thigh between her legs. The heat coming off her pussy warmed my leg through my jeans as I took her mouth with mine. Devouring her lips with my own, I let her feel all the passion I'd always had for her.

When she started tugging at my shirt, I broke the kiss and stepped away. Not far, just enough to rip my shirt off and undo my jeans. I fished a condom out of my pocket—because when I'd gotten dressed, I'd been optimistic about how this night was gonna end—before I shoved them down my thighs. I didn't bother even trying to take them all the way off. I was too desperate for her. I'd do her slow and steady later. Right now, I just needed to pound into her. Claim her. *Finally.*

The second I had that condom on, I had my hands on her waist, lifting her up the wall. With a gasp she wrapped her arms and legs around me, and I attacked her mouth as I thrust up into her hard and fast. Damn, she was so fucking tight. She'd tensed against me so I held still, enjoying the hell out of finally having my cock surrounded by her heat, as I continued to kiss her until her body relaxed. The moment she started to squirm against me, I let loose, taking her hard and fast like I needed to.

"So. Fucking. Good. Babe."

She moaned and tossed her head back against the wall. I buried my head in against her throat, nipping her skin. Shifting a palm up, I kneaded her tit, loving how the tip was hard for me and scraped against my skin. Her channel rippled around me and her nails bit into my shoulders as she grew close to coming. I couldn't fucking wait to see her come apart for me. Leaving her tit, I moved my hand down and pressed down on her clit.

"Come for me, Marie. Now."

Chapter 4

Marie

Looking into Scout's blue eyes, I allowed myself to fall over the edge. I screamed out his name as I clung to him and bucked against his thick erection as he continued to thrust in and out of me. My mind spun, my thoughts whirled together until nothing made sense. I was just starting to come back down when, with a growl, he thrust in deep then held still within me. His cock twitched deep inside me, which set off another round of sparks flying through my system.

When the storm finally passed, I flopped against him. Keeping my legs wrapped around his waist, I slung my arms around his shoulders as I dropped my head against his upper chest, my face up against his beard. My other hand I moved to play with the hair at the back of his neck. With a contented moan, I turned to kiss and nibble at his skin, loving the salty taste of him.

"Fuck, babe. I need more of you."

That had me chuckling. "I thought men needed some recovery time between rounds."

"Pretty sure when it comes to you, I'm not gonna ever need much time."

He wrapped one arm around my lower back while the other cupped my ass as he moved us away from the wall. I stayed relaxed against him, enjoying the way his skin felt against mine and the ease with which he carried me, while he strode across the room. When my back hit the bed, I released my hold on him and watched through hooded lids as he shed the rest of his clothes. A grin stretched my lips as he moved toward the bathroom. He'd been so hot for me, he'd not even bothered to fully strip. Not gonna lie, that shit was good on a girl's ego.

He had me licking my lips when he came back to me with a wet cloth, a hard body and a sexy grin. I opened my legs, and he proceeded to gently wipe me down before he tossed the cloth back in the direction of the bathroom.

"Such a gentleman."

He huffed out a breath and with a shake of his head, he slid onto the mattress on his side. I rolled over so we faced each other before I raised a hand to run my fingertips over his face. I trailed one over his eyebrow before I went down his nose, then I stroked his beard for a moment before giving it a light tug. It was so soft against my skin.

His hands weren't idle either. He stroked my body with gentle touches as he learned my curves. I wasn't a thin woman. Hell, I was turning forty-three tomorrow, and I had the padding to prove it. Not that I was obese.

Working in the cafe and being on my feet all day together with a healthy diet kept me fit. But it didn't stop the extra pounds around my middle from hanging around.

"You're so fucking gorgeous, babe."

I ran my fingers over his muscular chest as I responded. "You're not so bad yourself, Charlie."

He scoffed a laugh. "So, you do know my birth name. Who told you?"

I smirked at him. "I'm not at liberty to give up my sources. When did you earn your nickname?"

"I bet it was Bulldog, or Rose." I kept my face neutral, not giving away he had it right and it was Bulldog's wife, Rose who'd told me a long time ago. "Fine, you're not gonna tell me. My folks started calling me Scout when I was a young boy. Not entirely sure why, but it stuck. You know, I've always wondered how you ended up in foster care to begin with?"

"The usual. My mother liked drugs more than me. No idea who my father is." I shrugged and shook my head a little. "Strange how we've known each other for so long, yet we know so little about each other."

"Yeah, well, I was being a stubborn fool. Those days are over now. Marie, this right here? It's me claiming you for good. You're my old lady, now and forever."

As I lay there trying to form a response, he rolled over on top of me and fused his mouth to mine to kiss me senseless again. Tangling my hands in his hair, I gave over and enjoyed finally having Scout all to myself. I still wasn't one hundred percent sure on his declaration that he was claiming me for good. After twenty-five years of him pulling me in and pushing me away, it was going to take more than a few pretty words to make me believe it.

Leaving my mouth, he trailed kisses down my throat, his beard tickling me as he went and making me giggle. He gave me a low growl before he turned my laughter into a gasp when he took a nipple in his mouth and gave it a hard suck. My grip in his hair tightened as he moved to give the other side the same treatment. Every suck and nip he made sent a shock wave directly to my clit and I ground my pelvis up against his. Wanting, needing more.

"You on birth control?"

I shook my head. "Never needed to worry about it."

I winced when he lifted his head to stare into my eyes. Maybe I should have just lied to him. Now he was going to ask more questions. I just knew it. My body began to cool off as my gaze got trapped by his intense blue irises.

"How many lovers have you had, Marie?"

That had me cringing, but for some reason I couldn't break eye contact.

"Counting you just now, two."

With my breath held, I watched as he frowned for a moment before he tilted his head and confusion spread over his expression.

"You've only had one lover since you moved out of my house all those years ago?"

My cheeks heated with a mix of anger and embarrassment as I nodded my head, technically my first time had been before I moved into his house, but I wasn't going to point that out right now.

"Well, it's not like your damn club made it easy for me to date! Every time a man showed any interest, he'd get chased off!"

I tried to shove him off me but the bastard didn't move.

"I'm sorry." I froze at his words and he cleared his throat. "I had no idea my boys were pulling that shit with you. Bulldog mentioned something to me yesterday about it going on, and honest to God, that was the first I knew of it."

"That doesn't make it better, Scout! It doesn't all go away now because you didn't order it. It's still on you and the Charons that my life has passed me by and I've got nothing to show for it!"

He moved up so his face was level with mine. Holding his weight on one arm, he cupped my face with his other hand.

"Babe, you could have moved at any moment. You could have said something to me about it. But you didn't. Why?"

I closed my eyes against his intensity, my anger and heat fading. He was right, it was equally my decision to stay in Bridgewater. I knew the Iron Hammers would have completely forgotten all about me and Sarah within a few months. I could have followed Sarah and moved on, but I hadn't. Like some stupid, lovesick fool, I'd stayed.

"You know why I stayed."

"Need to hear the words, babe."

Another healthy dose of anger and embarrassment buzzed through me, and I glared up at him.

"Because I'm a fucking idiot. Because for twenty-five fucking years, I've been waiting for you to pull your head out of your ass and see me. Really see me. And all that got me was a few moments of hope, where you'd give me some fucking attention, affection, only for you to shut down on me again afterwards. It didn't give me a family, or love, or someone to keep me warm and safe at night. Nope, it's given me nothing but pain and heartache. Thanks for the reminder. Now, get *off* me!"

With my final words I shoved at his shoulders as hard as I could and he rolled to the side. It was enough for me to get out from under him, to rush to the bathroom where I shut and locked the door. Then I stalled out. My chest was on fire with pain. Once again I'd allowed that man in, only to have him rip me open. Stumbling over to the sink, and with a hand on the cool surface on either side of it, I let my head hang as the tears dripped from my eyes. Soon sobs wracked my body, making me shudder to the point my knees grew weak. I was so lost in my misery, I didn't hear when Scout managed to unlock the door.

"Ah, fuck, babe."

I just shook my head. I was too far gone to speak, and I didn't have anything left to say. What could I say? That I was in the middle of a full-on midlife crisis and he'd asked the exact wrong question and set off all my internal triggers? Somehow I didn't think that would help matters.

Scout

Fucking hell. What had I done to this beautiful, strong woman? How could I have been so fucking selfish to not have seen what my actions were doing to her all these years?

I stayed on the bed in a state of shock until I heard her first sob. Cringing, I hopped up and rushed over to the door. Naturally she'd locked it, but it was the type of handle that had a release on it, you just needed a coin or screwdriver. Going over to my jeans I pulled out my Leatherman, grateful I'd decided to bring it with me, and flipped out the flat head screwdriver as I went back to the door. In seconds I had the lock popped open. After quickly tossing the Leatherman back on my jeans, I shoved the door open and stopped dead in my tracks.

She was leaning over the sink, her shoulder-length hair hiding most of her face, but I could still see in the mirror the tears that were dripping from her face into the sink. Her whole body shook with her sobs. Fucking broke my heart that I'd done this to her—the one woman in this world who meant the most to me—and I'd fucking broken her.

"Ah, fuck, babe."

Her knees wobbled but she caught herself before she crashed to the floor. *Enough of this shit.* I rushed forward and lifted her, cradling her against my chest. She wrapped her arms around my neck and resting her head on my shoulder, she buried her face in against my beard as she continued to cry. I made my way back to the bed, and holding her with one arm, I shoved the bedding aside, then climbed in so I was sitting with my back against the headboard. Marie gripped me tighter, like she was afraid I was gonna put her down. Not fucking likely. I would never put her aside again if I could help it.

Leaning forward, I grabbed the blankets and sheets and pulled them up so they covered her trembling body and just held her, stroking her back until the storm passed. My chest fucking ached at the pain I'd caused her. As her sobs began settling down, I pressed a kiss to the top of her head and decided there was no point in trying to talk things out tonight. She was too tired and emotional.

As smoothly as I could manage, I shifted down the bed until I could lie down. Without a word, Marie shifted so her body was pressed up against mine. Her thigh over mine, her arm over my torso and her head nestled into the indent below my shoulder. Glancing down, I lifted my hand to move the hair out of her face and tuck it behind her ear. Fuck, she was beautiful. Even with tear streaks down her face, she was the most gorgeous woman I'd ever seen.

"Go to sleep, babe. In the morning I'll make it right. We'll fix this."

She tensed for a moment, but stayed silent and kept her eyes closed. I kept up stroking her back and face gently, until she was sound asleep. Then I let myself follow her into dreamland, hoping like fuck we could talk and fix things in the morning.

When I woke, I rolled to the side and threw out my arm for Marie, but only found cold sheets. Sitting up, I held my breath and glanced around the room for any sign of her. I couldn't hear the shower running, and when I noticed my clothes were neatly hanging over the back of a chair, and there was nothing else in the room, I realized she'd left. She'd woken before me and snuck out. Anger coursed through my veins as I tore the sheets back and quickly dressed. Leaving her room, I stormed down the hall to my own room and made fast work of getting changed and packing my bag. Even though I knew she wouldn't answer my call, I pulled my cell out and hit up her number. It rang for-fucking-ever before clicking over to voicemail, but I didn't leave a message. I didn't know what to say. Nope, I'd head back to Bridgewater and go see her tomorrow at her cafe. Head in after the lunch rush, and make sure Zara was around to close up so I could take her away somewhere.

Checking out thankfully didn't take long, then I was back at my bike. Storing my bags, I pulled my Charons cut out and put it back on. Then took a deep breath. It had felt strange not wearing it last night. But Marie had wanted a biker-free weekend, and I'd wanted to give it to her. Pulling my pack of smokes out, I got one lit up and took a few long drags before I started my bike and put my helmet on. Once I finished my smoke, I crushed the butt under my boot, tossed it in a nearby can, then got on my Harley and rode out of town.

The entire ride back home, my head was a tangled mess of thoughts. I wasn't paying attention like I should've been, which was how I found myself being boxed in as I neared Bridgewater. A large van behind, beside and in front of me, meant I was fucked. No way could I go off road. I'd wreck my bike, and no doubt injure myself so I couldn't fight off whoever this was that was fucking stupid enough to touch a Charon. I slowed down as they did until we all came to a stop. Staying on my ride, I reached down and pulled my gun out, flicking the safety off, as I waited for these fuckers to come get me.

When I heard car doors open on the vehicle behind me as well as in front, I moved off my bike so I had a better line of sight on all the vans. I'd never seen any of the half dozen men who approached me before.

"What the fuck do you bastards want? Because this is not the way to get shit outta the Charons."

"I beg to differ, Scout. I think my way is an excellent way. But we're not doing it out here. Say goodnight, *prez*."

Fuck. I spun to look behind me but was too late. One of the fuckers had snuck up behind me and stabbed a needle into my neck before I could react. I raised my gun and got two rounds off, hearing the grunts as they hit home, before whatever they gave me kicked in and I hit the pavement.

Chapter 5

Marie

Monday morning I had to drag myself into my cafe. I was so damn tired. Scout had rung me once Sunday morning and when I'd not answered, he hadn't left a message. The fact he hadn't tried to contact me at all since left a sour taste in my mouth—and a damn ache in my chest. When would I learn?

"Holy shit, Marie! What the hell happened in Houston? I thought you were going to relax and get pampered, and well, the new outfit looks great, but you look like someone ran over your cat. And I know you don't have one, so it can't be that."

My lips twitched up in a small smile as Zara came in the door, mouth running already.

"I was having a lovely time until Scout rocked up."

The younger woman winced. "Yeah, sorry about that. Mac asked why I was opening for you, and ah, I guess I didn't think. Just told him the truth, then he went flying out the door. Men." She came up and wrapped her arms around me. "Seriously, are you doing okay? I can get

Mac to go hit him upside the head for you? He'll do it. Everyone loves you, Marie."

I returned her hug, before I moved away a little.

"Don't worry about it, sugar. All those boys always tell their president every damn thing. It's always been like that. Scout was like that before he became the president. And I'll be fine. He just did what he always does, pulled me close only to push me away again." I let out a sigh, I hadn't meant to say that much. "C'mon, let's get ready for the day. People still need to eat and drink."

Zara looked like she wanted to say more, but she thankfully didn't. Considering Zara's reaction to seeing me, I paused in getting everything set up to make myself a coffee. Hopefully it would be enough to perk my ass up for the day. I was taking my last mouthful when the front door crashed open, hard enough to rattle the windows.

"What the fuck?"

I didn't tell Zara off for swearing in the cafe, mainly because I was thinking exactly what she'd said and then when I saw who it was, I was too shocked to care.

"Sarah?"

Dressed in a simple cotton dress, messy hair and what looked like a bruise forming around her throat, my foster sister stood leaning back against the door, her eyes wild.

"Thank God I found you! Marie, we gotta talk. No, we gotta go. Like now. We'll talk on the way."

She was speaking so fast, I could barely understand her. I went to her and pulled her away from the door and into a hug. I could barely believe she was really here!

"Come into the back room and tell me what the hell's got you so riled up, because I can't just up and leave my business for no good reason."

As I guided her through the shop, she continued to mumble. I shouted out to Zara to call Mercedes in. I had a feeling this wasn't going to be a quick visit.

"No time, no time."

Ignoring her words for the moment, I didn't stop until I had her safely out of sight in the back room, where I sat her down before sitting across from her at the little table.

"Right, Sarah, you're not making a lick of sense right now. Take some deep breaths and tell me what on earth has you running in here like your tail's on fire after over twenty years of silence."

She winced and closed her eyes as she took a deep breath. When she reopened her eyes, she reached for my hands, gripping them tightly.

"I didn't stay away by choice, sister. I fell down a rabbit hole worse than the Iron Hammers. But that's not important right now. They have Scout. They're hurting him. You have to come with me. We can sneak in, free him and sneak back out the way I did.

Not sure what to make of her words, I focused on her neck.

"Who hurt you?"

She shook her head. "It's not important! Scout doesn't have long, we gotta go!"

"No, we don't. That sounds dangerous, I'll call the club and they'll send a crew out there. Where are they holding him?"

It was taking all my strength to not fly into a panic. I really didn't want to believe her about Scout. Surely it was false? Would Sarah try to lure me into a trap of some kind, using my feelings for Scout against me?

"There isn't time for that. And if a bunch of bikers turn up, they'll just kill him. The best chance we have is to sneak in the way I got out. Do it ourselves."

"Sarah, I'm going to be honest here. Did whoever hurt you make you come here? To get me to come with you as bait or something?"

Her eyes widened, like she hadn't even thought of that.

"I don't think so. I was sneaking around the compound just after dawn because things were too quiet. It was odd. And I found the room they're holding Scout in. He's been tortured, Marie. He doesn't deserve that, not after all he's done to help us." She shook her head and tears filled her eyes. "He caught me. Nearly choked me, telling me how stupid I was, then he threw me out of the room and slammed the door in my face. I managed to slip out after that. We have to save him, Marie!"

Shit. Shit. *Shit.* What choice did I have? I couldn't leave Scout to be killed when the Charons stormed the place. I rubbed at my chest as the ache in my heart grew more painful. Was that why he hadn't called again? Because he couldn't? Wanting some kind of confirmation, I pulled my phone out and dialed Scout's cell. It went straight to voicemail. Dread cemented in my gut as my thoughts began to spin. We needed to go and save him, but it didn't feel right to go without at least letting the Charons know. I glanced to the doorway into the shop and saw Zara standing there listening in, looking worried. She held her phone up and I gave her a nod, which she returned. She'd let Mac know, and all the club would know within five minutes.

"Okay, Sarah. Let's do this. How'd you get here?"

"On foot. You have a car, right?"

With a nod, I snatched up my keys, phone and handbag before I headed for the front door. As I pushed through the doorway I glanced back and saw Zara frowning over at me while she was on the phone. Blinking back tears, I took a deep breath and pushed on, hoping like hell it wasn't the last time I would walk out of my cafe.

The drive out of town was quiet, except for Sarah giving me directions. I appreciated she didn't try to chat the whole way. Somehow I was managing to stay calm on the outside, but inside I was screaming. Just because Scout had pissed me off with what he'd said on the weekend, it didn't change the fact I loved the man. I began sending up prayers that he was okay, that we'd both get out of this alive.

Something about Sarah still had me on edge, like she wasn't telling me the whole truth. And I knew full well how that kind of shit could get you into trouble.

However, knowing that the Charons weren't going to be too far behind us, helped me keep my grip on my sanity. Who'd have thought I'd ever be grateful that Keys could track any one of us via our phone any time he wanted?

The further we went out of town, the more nervous I got.

"How much further is it? I don't think it's a good idea to park too close."

"Not far now, and yeah, announcing our arrival isn't going to help us."

A few minutes later, she directed me into a little convenience store on the outskirts of town. The lot only had a few other cars in it, and thankfully, no people were hanging around out here. Grabbing my bag, I popped the trunk and dumped it inside before locking up my car. Last thing I needed to be worrying about was my damn bag while doing this thing. I quickly checked my phone and saw a message from Zara saying the boys would be on their way soon. I deleted the message, just in case someone got hold of my phone, and because my paranoia was working overtime right now.

"Sarah, what kind of place are we going to? A house? Warehouse?"

"It was an old ranch house, but it's been extensively renovated and added onto. I think Bruce's folks were some kind of doomsdayers, or something."

I didn't ask anything else. But unease had the hairs on my neck tingling. How could she have lived here for over twenty years and not know things like that for sure?

She shook her head. "I'm sorry, my memory isn't the greatest. I often forget things..."

She trailed off as she started walking and I followed her. Maybe she was on drugs of some kind? Although, after what the Iron Hammers did to us, I couldn't believe she'd even consider doing drugs. Regardless, Sarah was someone I'd have to worry about later. Scout needed to be my first priority right now.

Scout

Gritting my teeth against the pain, I stayed silent as the fucker kneeling in front of me put another slice over my ribs.

"Just tell us what we want to know, then we can sort out a deal and stop this shit."

I glared at the asshole who was standing back watching me be tortured, pretending like he cared. It had been like this from the moment I woke up strung up from this fucking hook like a slab of beef. My bare feet barely touched the ground, and my arms had gone numb before I woke up so I didn't have the ability to lift up and kick out at the bastards. I'd tried, but just couldn't get my muscles to do what I fucking wanted them to.

To start with, they'd tried to beat information out of me about the bunker and what it was being used for, until they figured out that wasn't going to get them anywhere. I'd been in the Marines for years, and since returning to

Bridgewater, had always enjoyed a regular good round or two in the ring set up behind the club's gym. A beating I could take, no matter how hard they wailed on me. This cutting shit they were doing now though, that stung like a motherfucker. The thin, sharp blade sliced through my flesh like it was fucking butter. Nothing deep, because even they seemed to know a dead man couldn't talk. But they were getting as annoying as fuck. The feel of my blood trailing down my body wasn't great either. They'd stripped me from the waist up before I woke up. They'd also taken my boots and socks off, but had thankfully left my jeans alone so far. Although, I was sure they'd work up to that at some point. I still wouldn't tell them a fucking thing, though.

"I ain't telling you shit, and I sure as fuck ain't negotiating any kind of deal with fuckers who tie me up to beat the shit outta me, then try to fucking cut me like I'm some kind of steak."

At my words the boss man's face went red and he finally broke from his fake calm bullshit he'd been pulling. Lunging forward, he landed his fist right over my kidney. I'd expected it, and braced for it, but it still hurt like a motherfucker. Breathing through the pain, I did my best to keep my face neutral. I didn't want to give this asshole *anything*. Clearly he didn't like my stoic demeanor, as he stormed out of the room cursing me under his breath. Not sure what outcome he expected from this little stunt, but I was USMC trained, dammit. And I'd been president of the Charon MC for a long fucking time. I was no pushover, I would never spill my secrets, and I sure as hell didn't cave to little shits on a power trip. And that's what this was. He'd said something about us using his daddy's bunker to make money and he deserved a cut of it. My brain wasn't doing logic real well just at the moment, but I guessed this had something to do with the Satan's Cowboys and what they were doing over at the bunker on the gun range. In which case, it didn't matter what the fuck I said, I had no power over what Viper and his club did there. I'd told him no drugs on the streets of Bridgewater, and he'd agreed but that was pretty much the end of my control over that shit. So all this was for nothing, unless it was something else they really wanted. Because honestly, all this shit seemed a little excessive for some information about gun and drug running.

No matter what they were really after, these fuckers would kill me before they got anything. And if they did end me, hell would rain down on them like they'd never imagined. My brothers would call in the Cowboys and they'd all storm this place and fucking destroy every single one of them. In fact, as soon as my boys realized I was missing, Keys would find some way to track me here, then they'd come do that regardless. With or without back up from the Cowboys. The Charons were no pussies. If all my brothers showed up together, we'd get this place cleaned out and ended in no time. Fuck, I hoped he found a way soon. I really didn't want to fucking die here, especially with Marie still angry with me. An image of her pretty face filled my vision as the bastard who'd been cutting me moved away from me, following his boss out the door. Closing my eyes, I let my head hang forward, mentally going over every inch of my woman's face and body. Fuck, what I wouldn't give to be back in that hotel room in Houston with her. I should have tied her to the fucking bed before I went to sleep, to make sure she was still there when I woke up.

I kicked myself for not leaving a voicemail message. I should have at least wished her a happy birthday. If I died here, the last contact between us was me fucking hanging up on her. Even though I'd fucked up and said things that had hurt her, would she realize in time that I really did care about her? Fuck, she'd been the moon and stars in my world for over twenty fucking years. No one I'd fucked since meeting her had meant a damn thing because she'd had my heart. A shudder ran through my body as I remembered how it had felt to slide inside her heat for the first time. Finally. Fuck, I was such a damn fool for wasting so many years.

Her scent filled my nose a moment before I heard her voice.

"Ah, hell, Scout."

Was this a dream? I shook my head to clear it before I opened my eyes and sure enough, Marie was standing in front of me, her palms reaching for my face. *Definitely a dream.* I hissed in a breath when she touched me, her skin so warm and soft against my face. She leaned in and pressed the lightest kiss to the side of my mouth, like she

was scared she'd hurt me. It didn't matter if I was
dreaming, I needed to tell her everything I hadn't earlier.

"Love you, babe. I'm so fucking sorry I screwed
things up. I get crazy possessive about you. Even the
thought of you ever having been with someone else
drives me fucking nuts. Forgive me, yeah?"

Her expression softened as she stroked my face again.
"You're forgiven, but how about we get you out of here
before we have a big heart to heart?"

Frowning, I shook my head. She was nothing but a
hallucination. She couldn't be here. "Out of where,
babe?"

Her eyes grew wide before she turned from me and
looked around the room. Someone else behind her passed
her a bottle which she made fast work of uncapping and
holding up to my mouth. I opened for her to pour the
liquid in, not really expecting to get any. My imagination
wasn't that good.

Cool, clean water flowed into my mouth and I
swallowed that shit down as fast as I could. Fuck, I was
so damn thirsty. She pulled it away before I was done and
I growled.

"No, Scout, you'll make yourself sick."

"You're fucking really here. Are you crazy, woman?
Go! Get outta here while you still can."

Oh fuck, they'd come back and find her here. She
couldn't take the abuse they'd dealt out to me, it'd break
her. I tugged on my arms, trying to break free as she
searched the wall behind me for something.

"Don't suppose you know how to release your hands? I can't find anything that would lower you down."

They'd wrapped my wrists in chain, then attached it to a hook that hung down from the ceiling. I was sure there was a lever somewhere, but I had no fucking clue where it was.

"I'll look outside the room."

"No, Sarah, don't—"

Oh fuck, the other woman was Sarah? Marie's foster sister? I didn't have time to ponder that thought for long as Sarah was brought back in by the head asshole. He had his hand wrapped up in her hair, while the other held a wicked looking hunting knife against her throat.

"Well, looks like my little mouse came home and brought a friend." Marie shuffled until she stood directly in front of me, pressing her back to my front. I took deep breaths, breathing her scent in as I prayed to anyone who'd listen that she wouldn't be hurt by these bastards. "You must be Marie? Yes, no need to answer. I'd hoped when Sarah found we held her savior that she'd go running to get you. I do so love when plans work out, don't you?"

What the hell was he talking about now? How the hell did Sarah fit into all this shit? The water had helped clear my head. Fuck, who was I kidding, having Marie in danger was what had cleared the fog from my head so fast. Had my woman really come storming in here with no backup? I was gonna spank her ass red when we got out of here. Putting herself in danger like that... but first, we had to fucking get out of here, somehow.

The fucker kicked the door shut, and I heard the lock slide home. Dammit. That wasn't a good fucking sign. At least he was on his own. Keeping his back facing away from me and Marie, he moved over to the opposite wall where he briefly turned away from us and made fast work of shackling Sarah up to the wall. Unlike me, her arms weren't fully extended, but it still wouldn't take long for her arms to start hurting at the angle he had them.

"I guess now we're all here I can tell you what this is really all about. Because, I'm guessing as soon as I get to work on the lovely Marie here, you're gonna tell me every damn thing I wanna know, aren't you Scout?"

"Leave her the fuck alone. She's got nothing to do with this!"

Fury had me vibrating and I wanted nothing more than to be set free so I could shove Marie behind me and take this fucker out with my bare fucking hands.

"You had your chance for that. You chose to not talk, so here we are. Not that I'm complaining. I've waited a *long* time to be able to fully play with these two. Of course, I've been fucking around with little Sarah here for a good, long while, she just doesn't realize it." He ran a finger down her cheek, dragging moisture from her tears before he moved to grab her breast roughly. "You got no fucking clue we've been testing drugs on you all this time, do you little mouse? Ever wonder why you wake up in the mornings so very sore? No? Hmm, we still have some tweaks to make. It seems they mess with memory more than we need it to."

Bile rose in my throat, but I forced it down, and tugged on my arms again. Pain flared through the numbness but I didn't care. I couldn't believe what this fucker was saying he'd been doing. And how in the hell did Sarah get mixed up with him and his shit in the first damn place?

Chapter 6

Marie

I could barely process what he was saying. He'd been drugging and using Sarah as a whore for however long he'd had her? And the drugs he'd pumped her full of had screwed her memory up? What the hell kind of rabbit hole had we'd all fallen down? Scout was seething with anger, I could feel it radiating off him. Reaching back, I put my palms on his sides, trying really hard to not focus on the stickiness I came into contact with. They'd tortured him, cut little slices into his torso, in a pattern up his ribs.

The bastard, who I guessed must be Bruce, turned away from Sarah, who was now shaking with her sobs. "Nope, I'm gonna enjoy working you both over, but good. Because you see, when you two got away from the Iron Hammers all those years ago, you left others behind didn't you?" He didn't give me time to answer, "Yeah, that's right. You left all those other women behind, to be drugged and used however those fuckers felt like—"

My temper got the better of me, and I interrupted. "How is that any different than what you've done to Sarah? For how long?"

He grinned an evil smile. "That's the point, Marie. She's been used as my sister was. She's been paying the price you soon will for leaving others behind. And it's been a good, long while—about twenty-three years, I believe. Poor little Sarah, she was so scared of bikers, even her saviors, the Charon MC. When I came along and offered her sanctuary here away from society in general, she jumped at the chance. For a girl who grew up in foster care, she really is surprisingly gullible."

Yeah, she was. That's why I'd always looked out for her. I hated that she up and left Bridgewater like she had. But I hadn't wanted to go, so I let her make her choice and leave.

"I guess you'd have called my father a doomsdayer. He prepped for the end of the world. A little too much, in my opinion. It meant that like Sarah, my sweet sister grew up very naive and unaware of the evils in the world. When she rebelled and ran away, father sent me to retrieve her. But she'd vanished. I couldn't find her anywhere locally. So I came home to tell father. After that he went a little crazy—well—a little *more* crazy. My mother had died giving birth to my sister, so we were all the old man had. It took him over a year to finally locate her. She'd been picked up by one of the Iron Hammers and taken to their clubhouse... but you two know all about how that works, don't you? How they drug and rape those girls until they're completely hooked on that shit they pump into them all the damn time. By the time father tracked her that far, she'd already been moved on. You see, my sister was a pretty thing. Blonde hair, blue eyes, fair skin, not a mark on her precious body. Father found her in a brothel over the border in Mexico. I went with him down there, and we were loaded to start a fucking war to get her back."

He paused to stalk toward me, I swallowed nervously as he got closer. There was no point in trying to run, the door was shut and locked. He wrapped his palm around the front of my throat and squeezed just enough that I felt a little restriction on my breathing. Scout's growl filled the room as I raised my hands to try to pry his hand from me, but he held firm and ignored my efforts.

"When those Mexican assholes realized who we'd come for, they slit her throat and tossed her out the door to land at our feet. We barely recognized her. What they'd done to her." His eyes glazed over for a moment with moisture, as though he really had loved his sister. "Father went into warrior mode. I tried to stop him but he wouldn't listen, he went barging in there with guns blazing. He took out a good half dozen men before he was killed."

"We didn't do any of that. You know we didn't! I've told you what happened that night, how we got told the police were in the Iron Hammers' pocket and wouldn't have helped those other girls. We were just kids ourselves."

Sarah's voice was hoarse with emotion and if I could talk, I was sure mine would be the same. Guilt over not doing anything to save those other girls had eaten away at me constantly since that night.

"As soon as we found out what the Iron Hammers were doing, we went down there together with the Iron Wolves MC and shut that shit down. New management down there now and all the girls they still had have been put through rehab and given all the help they need to get back on their feet. When you'd realized who'd taken your sister, you should have come to us. We didn't fucking know back then what they were up to, dammit."

Scout's words seem to make him even angrier. With a growl, he tossed me aside and I went crashing into the wall with the force of his shove. Fuck that hurt. I'd managed to turn enough my shoulder caught the brunt of the hit, but still. Ouch. I glanced back over just as the bastard landed a fist against Scout's cut up side. I winced even as Scout stayed stoic.

"Why the hell would we have gone to an MC to deal with another MC? You would have sided with them. I know how you bastards are all about brotherhood. And don't fucking lie to me! You had to know after the girls were given to you."

"They never told me exact details. And we only back up another MC when it's deserved. Anyone in this corner of Texas knows if you have an issue with the Iron Hammers, the Charons are the ones to come see about it. Nothing you do here will bring back your sister or father.

I'm sorry you lost them, but this isn't fixing it. What you've done to Sarah for over twenty fucking years, isn't going to bring them back. Stop this shit now, before it costs you your life."

Crazy bastard threw his head back and laughed. "It ain't me that's gonna lose my life here today. That honor is all yours. Then I'm gonna use your woman just like I have Sarah. I'm sure my men will appreciate the fresh meat."

I could see Scout was struggling to keep his rage under wraps.

"This was never about that fucking bunker, was it?"

I had no idea what Scout was talking about, but I made the most of them talking and shifted so I could slowly rise from the floor where I'd landed.

"Of course not. That was just to get the others on board to help me snatch you, and in turn, Marie. They don't know shit about who was responsible for what happened to my sister. How these two bitches left her to be used and sold to be used some more. Nor do they realize an MC would never give a civilian a fucking cut of their business. I'm not stupid, I just needed an excuse to get the others to help me."

"And the drugs? How many are in on that shit?"

"Only a few. Can't trust many people these days. But that's all good. Less ways to split the money once we get it right, and none of the men complain when Sarah turns up high as a kite and looking for some cock. They don't give a shit what she's on, so long as she willing to spread her thighs, or open her mouth. Sure they'll love it even more when there's two of them to use."

Trying not to gag at what he was saying, I made the most of the fact his focus was so completely on Scout, he didn't notice me moving. Taking a deep breath, I moved around the perimeter of the room, as quietly as I could manage. When I reached Sarah, I waited for him to say something else—do something to cover the noise I was going to make by flipping open the shackles. Thankfully, he hadn't taken the time to lock them with anything other than basic clips.

"Don't you dare fucking touch either of them!"

As Scout roared out his words, I flipped open the latches and Sarah fell against me for a second.

"I'm so sorry, I didn't know this was a trap."

Worried her whispered words would gain his attention, I shook my head. "Shh, I know. Everything will be okay."

Then I held a finger to my lips as the stupid bastard kept up his rather descriptive lecture on all that he planned on doing to me and Sarah. Bile churned in my gut. This was a very sick man, indeed.

Taking a quick look around the room, I tried to find a weapon but came up with no options. Instead, I found a lever. It had been behind the door, which was now shut. Would that free Scout? How quickly would it work? Dammit. Before I could come up with another plan, Sarah let out a scream and barreled into him. She'd pulled a knife from somewhere and had it buried in his stomach.

Bolting over to the lever, I used both hands to shove hard against the thing until it clunked up and I heard chain rattle as I spun back around to see Scout rushing to free his hands. Before he could, the asshole lifted Sarah with a roar and threw her against the wall. I screamed as my sister fell lifeless to the floor, then screamed again when the door came crashing open, barely missing me, and a flood of Charon brothers streamed into the room.

Shocked to my core, I bolted to Sarah and lowered down to the floor beside her.

"No, no, no."

Pressing my fingers against her wrist, I moved it around but couldn't find a pulse. Tears burned my eyes then flowed freely.

"C'mon, luv. Let me take a look."

Taz, with his familiar Aussie accent in my ear, gently gripped my shoulders and moved me over until he could get in to touch Sarah. But I knew the truth. She was gone. I'd failed to look after her. Hell, I should have taught her more about the world. Given her the skills to avoid falling for shit like this. Before Taz could confirm her death, I buried my face in my hands and set my emotions free. I cried for Sarah, for that asshole's sister, for all the girls the Iron Hammers had destroyed. It was all more than I could handle. I could hear Taz trying to talk to me but I was too far gone, so I just shook my head as I kept sobbing.

Scout

Everything happened so fast. I was still reeling from what this bastard had told me when I'd seen Marie creeping toward Sarah, so I'd yelled out to give her the cover she needed to free her friend. But after that, everything went to fucking hell. I'd stopped listening to the fucker in front of me as he tried to rile me up with everything he planned to do to my woman. I knew he wouldn't live long enough to do any of it. No fucking way. I refused to believe anything else.

I kept my gaze on the man in front of me, but I was focused on the women in my peripheral vision. Marie had moved over to behind the door, to where a lever was. It took all my self-control to not hold my breath in hope. Then with a scream, Sarah lunged at her tormentor. She'd pulled a knife from somewhere, her boot maybe? And when he turned to face her, she buried that thing deep in the fucker's gut. Marie must have thrown the lever because the hook came rushing down and I shifted fast to avoid the chain landing on my head. Finally able to stand flat footed, my feet and legs came alive with tingles of pain as I tried to free my hands so I could take down the fucker before he could do any more damage, but I wasn't fast enough. My arms and hands were more useless than my damn legs. Sarah was a tiny wisp of a girl and even injured, he had no trouble lifting her, then with a roar he threw her hard against the wall. With a crunch, she fell lifeless to the floor. *Fuck.* It was then that the door burst open and my brothers arrived. Arrow, Nitro, Mac, Taz and Eagle. I'd never been happier to see them.

Taz went over to where Marie was crouched near Sarah, while the other four came to me. Nitro kicked the back of the asshole's knees and he went down. With his gut injury rapidly weakening him, he kept going until he was lying on the concrete. Mac helped unwrap the fucking chain until I had my hands free. Pain, like liquid fire shot through my arms but I gritted my teeth and tried to push it down.

"Scout, I need you to clench and unclench your hands a couple times for me."

I followed Mac's instructions and was happy to see all my fingers did what they were fucking told. Hopefully I'd managed to not get any nerve damage from this clusterfuck. I needed my hands to ride and work on bikes in the shop. And to love on Marie.

"I'm fine. Let me at him."

Mac shook his head but shifted out of my way. The little shit was groaning on the floor, clutching his gut. The wound would kill him, but not fast enough for my fucking liking.

"Go straight to hell, you fucking bastard."

With that I lifted my foot and kicked his head with the heel, hard enough we all heard the snap of his neck, even over Marie's sobs.

"Right, we need to move out. You bring the bus, yeah?" When they all nodded, I continued. "Great. I'm going to take Marie up to Donna, then we're cleaning house. Taz? Sarah breathing?"

"Yeah, but her pulse is weak. I don't want to move her, pretty sure she's got a spinal injury going on. We need to call in the professionals for her. It's the only way she'll live. Sorry, prez. I know you'd prefer just burn this place to the ground, but it's not what she needs."

I'd been certain the fucking asshole had killed Sarah when he'd thrown her against that wall. Guess not. But the woman wasn't moving, and Taz hadn't tried to shift her either. Although, with all things considered, death was probably the kindest outcome for the poor woman. What she'd been through all these years would be one hell of a thing to overcome. At least she'd gotten that blade into him, got some vengeance. I shook out my arms that were still fucking hurting. "Fine, call them in. I want everyone in this place rounded up, and I need to pick out the fuckers who were working with that asshole, then we'll leave the rest to the cops."

"That shouldn't take long, prez, we brought the whole club with us. The other brothers have been rounding up everyone while we came looking for your sorry ass."

I nodded at Arrow's words as I tried to make my way over to Marie, who was still crying like her soul was bleeding and it was breaking my fucking heart.

"Whoa, where do you think you're going?"

I turned to glare at Arrow as he caught me mid-stumble. "To my fucking woman. You got a problem with that?"

"As a matter of fact I do, prez. In case you weren't aware, we're in a fucking basement. That means stairs out of here. You wanna risk dropping her on your way out? You want to waste a shit ton of time getting your sorry ass out to the bus and not have time to do whatever the fuck it is you want to do with the others in this place before the cops turn up? Because you know as well as I do that the second we call that ambulance in, the cops will follow that bus out here."

That had me wincing. "No way to keep the cops out of this, is there?"

"Afraid not, prez. But we'll be fine. We've done nothing wrong here. They took you, we came got you back. The girls will back us up. As for the rest of these bastards, they've been contained. We didn't go on a murdering spree. Since we didn't know exactly what we were dealing with, we went with an initial plan to contain, not destroy."

"That's gonna change a little. This fucker has produced a drug that needs to never see the light of fucking day. I need to figure out who knows about the drug, and make sure they all die. And there's one other man that needs to fucking die. The bastard who cut me up. We got room to take him back with us? Wouldn't mind venting a little frustration on that little piece of shit."

Arrow chuckled darkly. "We brought cages, we'll get him gone before the cops turn up. Since you can't lift

Marie, hurry up and pick which one of us gets the job so we can get moving here."

I wanted growl and thump my chest. Dammit, she was my woman! But Arrow was right, I'd probably drop her if I tried to pick her up right now.

"Mac, she knows you best. You do it."

With that, Mac was fast on his feet. He scooped up Marie and when I raised my hand, he brought her to me so I could press a kiss to her forehead, tell her it would be all right. I didn't think she heard me though, she was lost to her sorrow. I wondered if she'd heard Taz say that Sarah was alive.

"Eagle, you stay and watch Taz's back, yeah?"

"Of course, prez."

As soon as Mac was out the door, we followed. Arrow stayed close to my side and didn't say a fucking word when I had to grip his damn arm to steady myself as I contended with the stupid fucking stairs. Didn't help I had bare fucking feet. I hated not going with Mac and Marie, but I had a job to do.

"Did someone find my boots and my fucking cut yet? If that bastard destroyed it, I swear, I'm gonna find a way to bring him back so I can kill him again."

"I've got it right here."

I turned to Nitro, who'd spoken. "Give it to me."

"You sure you want to get blood and shit all over it?"

"I'm the fucking president of the Charon MC, and I got shit to do. Shit I need to wear my fucking cut for."

Whatever got on it, would wash out. But I needed the strength wearing it gave me for what I needed to do right now. Nitro handed it over and Arrow discreetly helped me shrug into it. Damn, but I felt better already. Hated being without my cut. I planted my ass down on a seat to pull my boots on before I rose to stand again. I bit back the groan but fuck, I felt like I was about eighty years old.

"Right, brothers. Let's go find us some fuckers to kill."

We made our way out the rear of the building and found a nice line-up of men all kneeling like they were waiting on their executions. Keg, Tiny, Bash and Bank stood over them with guns drawn, ready to accommodate just that, should any of them move. Bulldog stood at the end of the group and I had to double-take to be sure I was seeing right. Was he holding a fucking kid?"

"Bulldog, who you got there?"

"Got me a little princess. Ain't that right, sweetheart?"

His voice was falsely calm and the little girl clung tightly to his cut, clearly scared out of her damn mind. Grateful my cut was covering most of the damage that had been done to me, I strode over to them—thank fuck my legs and arms seemed to have recovered already. I looked into her little face and bit back a curse.

"She's Sarah's daughter. Bulldog, get her out to the bus. If Marie's awake, tell her she's Sarahs. We'll take good care of her. You understand, darlin'? You're gonna be safe with us, okay?"

She gave me a shaky little nod and Bulldog rushed her off around the side of the house. I shook my head. A fucking child. Just what this mess needed.

I strolled down the line until I found the fucker who'd cut me up. With my hand on his throat, I lifted him to stand.

"What's the kid's name and are there any more?"

He rasped in a breath and I loosened my hold so he could speak.

"She's the only one."

"It's been over twenty years, how is there only one toddler?"

"Bruce thought she was past being able to have kids a few years back. Wanted to save money on birth control. Turned out he was wrong."

"And her name?"

I asked again, because I knew Sarah well enough to know she'd have named her daughter. When the bastard shook his head in the negative, my temper rose. These bastards couldn't be bothered learning the name of the only child in the fucking place?

"Who's the fucking father?"

"No clue. Could be just about any one of us."

Fury coursed through me at what that poor woman had been put through. Guilt ate at me that I'd done such a fine fucking job of keeping her protected. Ron would be turning over in his grave right now.

"You know where the drug lab is?"

His eyes went wide but he refused to say a thing.

"Nitro? Take this little shit to go find that lab, and I want it burned to the ground. Nothing can survive that'll enable some other fucker to recreate that shit. We clear?"

"Crystal, prez."

"And, Nitro?" I waited for the man to look me the eye. "He's the one I told you about, yeah?"

His grin was dark. "Sure thing, prez."

Couldn't wait to have some fun with my new toy later. It'd been a while since I got a good workout in. Taz had the fun of working over the last fucker we had visit our basement.

I turned back to the others.

"You know who the fuck I am?"

No one said a word, but I had their complete attention.

"I'm the motherfucking president of the Charon MC. And your leader decided it was a great idea to fucking kidnap me, then use me as bait to grab my woman. It's not by chance that my club was named after the Greek ferryman, who in the myths was the one who decided where he ferried the souls of the dead to. Either Hades or the Elysian Fields. Heaven or hell. Guilty or innocent. It was up to the Charon to decide. Now it's my turn to play Charon. How you answer my questions is gonna make a big fucking difference on how your day ends, get me? Now, who was involved in the drug production?"

Naturally no one offered up a confession, but clearly none of these boys played poker and between all of us watching we soon had four men admitting they were involved.

"Now, who here has taken advantage of Sarah while she was fucking hopped up on that fucking drug?"

This time it was easy to pick who was innocent. We ended up with just three men innocent.

"Bank, Jazz and Keg take these three and tie 'em up out front. They get to go with the cops. Make sure they know the score. You other fuckers, well, you're getting sent straight to hell to join your motherfucking leader."

I turned away when I heard someone coming and gave Bulldog a nod as he stopped next to me. With my arms crossed over my chest I watched as my brothers fired their weapons. Shots rang out loud in the quiet as each of these fuckers went to meet their maker.

"Nitro's rigged the lab up to blow, along with the rest of the house. He left me the switch before he took off to take your prize back to the clubhouse."

"The bus here for Sarah yet?"

I hadn't heard sirens, but I'd been more than a little preoccupied so could have missed it.

"Five minutes out, cops are about ten minutes behind them."

I nodded. "We have a little time then. Brothers, load these bastards into the house. The moment Sarah's out, we'll clear out and blow the fucking joint."

"You ain't helping with it, prez. You need to go see Donna and get patched up."

I went to tell Arrow to go fuck himself, but he stood before me with his arms folded like he was getting ready to fucking toss me over his shoulder or some shit.

"You know, some days you really piss me off, brother."

"Yeah, but you love me for it. Now, get moving before I gotta drag your ass out there."

With everything pretty much taken care of, my adrenaline was fading fast. It seemed to take forever to walk around the side of the house. Fuck me, but I was getting too old for this shit. By the time I made it out to the front of the property, I was grateful to see our bus sitting there all ready to go with Marie laying in the back on the stretcher, Sarah's little girl curled up beside her. One of the best things we ever did was trip out this tank of a van into an ambulance, even if the thing did come in handy way too often for my liking.

Keys and his old lady, Donna hopped down from the rear and rushed over toward me.

"Dammit, Scout, what the hell did you let them do to you?"

"Donna, it wasn't exactly like I had a choice. What's wrong with Marie?"

"She'll be fine. Just a little shock and a few scrapes and bruises, I had to sedate her to calm her down. The child seems physically fine, but she's refusing to talk. Bulldog told her that Marie was Sarah's sister and she willingly curled up against her and went to sleep herself. Guess Marie's motherly vibe is universal, huh?" She paused to shake her head, as though trying to clear it. "Now, lose the leather, I need to see what I'm dealing with."

Shrugging out of my cut, I passed it to Keys, but before I attempted to get myself up into the back of the bus, I froze. Marie and the little girl were on the stretcher.

"Yeah, we're kinda full but since you seem to be fine standing, I'll take a look at you out here quickly, then we'll head back into town. You can get sewn up at the hospital."

I blew out a breath. "Can't you just throw in some stitches now? I got shit to do."

"No, I can't just 'throw in some stitches.' Shit, Scout, you should know better than to even ask. Now, how about you shut up and let me do my job, yeah?"

Keys, along with Arrow, laughed as I grumbled under my breath about stubborn females. Not that it got me anywhere. She went back into the bus and started rummaging around for something when the professionals pulled up. Bulldog was on it and quickly had them following him inside.

By the time the door opened again and the paramedics came out with Sarah strapped to a board, Donna had cleaned up my cuts and had slapped a bandage on them to last until we got back into town.

"Scout? With the condition Sarah is in, I think it might be in your best interest to get Child Protection Services involved with her case. Even if Sarah survives, she's going to be in hospital for a good, long while. The little one will end up in foster care."

An icy chill ran down my spine. "No way in hell is that girl going to some strange foster home. She'll be going with Marie and me."

I glanced around at the brothers with me to see who I could put in charge of this shit.

"Arrow, brother. Remember that senator we dealt with a few years back?"

The senator's aide decided to beat and rape a young woman, then the good senator decided to buy his aide out of any trouble he might get into over it. We didn't agree with that outcome and took it upon ourselves to deliver the deserved justice on the fucker. The senator couldn't prove it was us, but he knew. Also knew he fucked up by covering for the little shit and now owed us. He also knew what we'd do to him if he didn't honor his debt to us.

"Yeah. Little hard to forget."

"I need you to go pay him a visit, take a couple of the brothers with you. I want paperwork done up before that little girl leaves hospital so she goes home with me and Marie to my place. Understood?"

"You sure that's a good idea, prez? Won't Marie want to take her to her place?"

"You ever seen her place? There ain't no room for a kid. And we can grease all the palms we want, we still gotta meet the requirements. My house is huge and has plenty of room. That'll do for now."

He cocked his eyebrow at me. "And it gets Marie in your house too, huh?"

"Brother, I am *not* in the mood for your crap right now."

With a smirk, he left to do his job. He was aptly named Arrow. He spoke direct and got to the point, always. Even when you didn't want or need him to.

Turning to the ambulance, I was relieved to see they'd finally stabilized Sarah enough that they were preparing to head out. I'd been mentally willing the ambulance to hurry up and get gone with Sarah since they'd arrived. I'd like to blow this place before the cops rocked up, but didn't want to risk further injuring the poor woman. Eagle exited the front door and headed directly to me.

"House is all clear, most of the boys have headed out now everything's done."

"Great, the second that bus is out the driveway, I want this shit blown."

Eagle glanced into our bus at the sleeping little girl.

"Can I suggest you get gone too? No need to traumatize that poor girl any more than she's already been."

I winced. I should have thought of that, dammit. The blast would scare the shit out of the poor kid. For about half a second, I considered letting them go on ahead while I stayed back, but leaving Marie while she was out and defenseless didn't feel right.

"Fine. Bulldog has the detonator. Double check no Charons are in there before you hit that switch. I don't want any friendly fire casualties here."

"Yes, prez."

With that I climbed into the back to sit beside the girls, then within moments things were closed up and we headed down the road. I was technically leaving a crime scene, but fuck, I was injured. And they should have gotten their asses out there faster if they wanted to talk to me that quickly. I knew Donald, the club's friend on the force would find me at the hospital later to ask questions, and really, with my injuries, they couldn't give me shit about not waiting for them.

Leaning my head against the side of the vehicle, I closed my eyes to rest a minute as we drove back toward Bridgewater. Fuck, it was going to be a fucking long couple days dealing with all this shit.

Chapter 7

Marie

My nose stung as I woke. The strong scent of antiseptic clued me in to my location even before I opened my eyes to see I was lying on a hospital bed. Well, I was lying more on Scout than I was on the bed, but he didn't seem to mind. I lifted the blanket and glanced down his torso. All he wore was a pair of black boxers, which revealed all his injuries. With all the blood gone, it wasn't as bad as I'd thought. A clean, white bandage was wrapped around his middle and I could see raised rows where stitches must be. He'd probably end up with a row of straight scars up his ribs, but I doubted he'd care about it. All the black and blue over him had me wincing. Poor Scout. They'd been thorough with beating him and I had no idea how he could stand me pressed up against so many of the bruises.

"Hey, babe."

His voice was rough, and oh, so sexy. It had a wave of warmth flowing through me, heating me up from the inside.

"Hey, yourself. How you feeling?"

"Like I got beat on and cut up, but it's all good. I've had worse, and they didn't break bones so it won't take long for me to heal up. And since I got to wake up with you in my arms, I'm calling it a win. How about you? Your shoulder okay?"

I rolled the joint in question to test it, and all I felt was a twinge of pain. "It's fine now. Guessing it'll bruise up, but it doesn't hurt." Suddenly all the emotion from our rescue hit me and my eyes teared up again. "Poor Sarah. I had no idea she'd ended up out there, living like that."

"We might be able to sneak you in to visit her if you want. She's got a hell of a long road ahead of her."

I tried to sit up but Scout held me to him so all I could manage was to push myself up on my arms a few inches.

"What do you mean? She died. I couldn't find a pulse."

He lifted a palm up to cup my face. "She's alive. Taz found a pulse, but we had to call the professionals in for her because we suspected she had a spinal injury. She's still in ICU, so I'm not sure exactly where things stand right now, but I know she was alive when she left the house."

Tears pricked my eyes and fell, again. "She's alive." I lowered my head so it rested on Scout's chest, my ear pressed against his skin so I could hear the strong beating of his heart. His fingers stroked through my hair, smoothing it back from over my face.

"When are we allowed to leave?"

"We're just chilling here, waiting for you to wake up. We got the all clear a while back. Donna had to give you a light sedative to calm you down. I hated seeing you like that, Marie. So fucking upset you could barely breathe."

His grip tightened on me as he pressed a kiss to the top of my head.

"Why are we in the same bed and not separate ones?"

"Because he's a stubborn bastard who wouldn't let you go."

I tried to turn to look at Bulldog, whose voice had come from the direction of the doorway, but apparently Scout still didn't want to let me go. I turned my face to look up at his.

"You know you have to let me go at some point, right? Or I'll end up peeing on you or something."

Bulldog laughed as Scout scowled at me. "Fine, I'll release you for a bathroom break, but you better make it fast."

With a shake of my head, I slid off the bed. By the time my feet hit the floor, Bulldog was right there by my side. Thankfully I didn't need his help, as I found myself steady on my feet as I plodded over to the bathroom. When I got to the door and saw the shower, I turned back to Bulldog.

"Don't suppose you could find me a change of clothes so I can get cleaned up?"

He gave me a little frown. "You don't feel light headed or faint at all?"

I shook my head. "I just need a shower to wash away all the filth and grime from that place. I'm sure I'll feel much better afterward."

He nodded and then handed me a bag I hadn't noticed he was carrying. "Zara went and packed you a bag, hoping you'd be out of this place today. She also said to tell you her and Mercedes have the cafe covered for however long you need them to so you don't need to worry about it."

With a smile I thanked him, took the bag and locked myself into the small bathroom. For a few moments I just leaned back against the door and took some deep breaths. I could hardly believe that Sarah was alive. I needed to go see her, check with her doctor on how she was doing and what needs to happen with her recovery.

Pushing off the door I used the toilet, then stripped down and flipped on the taps to run the water hot, after checking the nasty bruise on my upper arm and shoulder, the ring of grey around my throat from where Bruce had grabbed me caught my gaze. Unable to look away, I pressed my fingers against the bruising, assessing how bad it was. Tears threatened at how close I came to dying today, but I pushed them down. Bruce was the one who died and I was here, alive. I opened my bag and smiled because Zara had thought of everything. I took out my shampoo, conditioner and body wash then went back to adjust the shower before getting in.

It was probably thirty minutes before I came out of the bathroom, but I felt a hundred times better. The hot shower had done wonders, as had having a little alone time. I rather got the feeling I wouldn't get much of that now Scout had apparently decided he needed to be physically touching me as often as he could manage it.

I walked back into the room to see that Scout had already put on clean jeans and his boots, along with a black t-shirt. He was currently shrugging into his Charon's cut. He reached for his head, clearly looking for the bandana he normally wore and adjusted about two hundred times a day.

"You bring me a bandana?"

Bulldog shook his head. "Sorry, man, didn't even think of it."

I came up behind him and ran my palms over the large Charon MC back patch. The skull in the center had a bat-like wing coming from the right side, while the left side had an angel wing. Good and bad. Or rather, bad for good reasons. I didn't need to know the details to know the club would have cleaned house out at the compound before they left.

Scout slowly turned, wrapping an arm around my waist as he did. I pressed myself against his chest then with a smile reached up and ran my fingers through his graying hair.

"You know, I prefer you without the bandana. I can't run my hands through your hair if you hide it all the time."

Bulldog scoffed. "And on that note, I'm outta here. I gotta get back to, um, you know. She settled okay with

Rose and Donna, but completely panicked when Silk tried to get near her. I think it's the ink on her arm. Anyhow, she seems okay with me, so I'm gonna head back. Oh, and Sarah's not allowed visitors yet, they're still trying to get the swelling of her brain to go down. Doc said by morning we should be able to go in and see her. I'll see you two later."

Scout nodded but didn't say anything as Bulldog left. I wanted to ask about who Bulldog was talking about. Had there been another woman out there? Before I could speak, Scout cut in.

"So, you don't mind all the biker stuff anymore, huh?"

I was still stroking my palm over the raised stitching on the patch on his back, even though I couldn't see it anymore.

"It was never really about you being a biker, Scout. It was about how you kept holding me at arm's length, but had your whole club not letting anyone else get near me either. I was lonely, and sick to death of it. Who was Bulldog talking about?"

Scout moved his hands to hold my face, so I was forced to look up into his eyes.

"Things will be different now. I wasn't yanking your chain in Houston, I've claimed you. You're my old lady and that ain't ever gonna change. You believe that, don't you? Believe that I want you in my life, in my bed, every fucking day for the rest of our lives?"

Tears pricked my eyes. He looked so earnest. So damn serious.

"It's a lot of change in a short time, Scout. Give me a minute to catch up okay?"

With a growl he crushed my lips beneath his in a fiery kiss that melted me. I clung to his biceps, desperate for an anchor to help me stay on my feet. Then just as suddenly as the kiss started, Scout ripped his mouth from mine, ending it.

"If we had the time, I'd show you right fucking now how much I want you, how much you're mine. But we don't have the time right now. I got someone you need to meet."

My thoughts were spinning and I was panting as I tried to get myself under control. Scout nuzzled his cheek against mine, his beard tickling my neck.

I cleared my throat. "Ah, who do I need to meet? Is it who Bulldog was talking about?"

He pressed kisses to my jaw before standing back up.

"Yeah. When we were clearing out that place we found a child. A little girl. Can't be much more than two or three years old."

Suddenly a wash of cold flowed over me, like my blood had become ice water.

"She Sarah's?"

Scout nodded slowly and I tightened my grip on his arms so I'd stay standing when my knees threatened to go weak.

"What's her name?"

"No idea. Not sure she even has one. None of the men out there could tell us her name or who her father is, but she's the spitting image of Sarah. Well, that and there were no other women out there. So, she has to be Sarah's. She kind of met you when she rode to the hospital cuddled up against you in the back of the bus. We told her you were Sarah's sister, and she clung to you."

I released Scout and tried to head for the door, suddenly desperate to see this little girl. But he wrapped his arm around my waist and pulled me back against him.

"Wait a second, there's something else. She hasn't spoken. Not one word since we rescued her. The doctors are trying to work out if there's a medical reason for it, but we suspect it's from the trauma she's suffered in her life."

That had tears flowing. That poor little angel.

"It doesn't matter, she's family. And I won't abandon her."

He cupped my face, swiping my tears with his thumbs.

"You're a natural mother, and I cost you that because I'm a damn fool. I'm so sorry, Marie. Can you forgive me?"

I shook my head at his words, unsure if I heard him correctly. "It's not a done deal yet, I still have regular cycles. You really want a baby?"

"Never wanted one before, but with you? Hell yeah, I do."

I smiled up at him before rising on my tip toes to press a kiss to his lips before pulling back and giving his beard a small tug.

"We'll have to work on that later. I want to meet Sarah's daughter."

The whole time I followed Scout through the halls of the hospital I thought over his words. I'd always wanted a family of my own, but at forty-three, could I really handle pregnancy and everything that came with a newborn? Sure, Zara and Silk both seemed to be handling motherhood well, but they were at least ten years younger than me.

I was jerked out of my thoughts when Scout stopped in front of a brightly lit room in the children's ward.

"Here we are."

He held the door open so I could go in first. Nerves had my palms sweating and I wiped them on my jeans as I stepped into the room. She was on the floor, along with Rose and Bulldog, playing with blocks, but she was facing the door and at the sound of it opening she'd stopped playing to stare at the doorway.

"Hey there, sweetheart. My name's Marie, and I grew up with your mom."

I slowly made my way over to her, keeping a gentle smile on my face. I didn't want to startle her. "I'm sorry I wasn't awake in the ambulance earlier. I would have given you cuddles if I had been."

She chewed on her lip and glanced to Bulldog. He ruffled her hair softly. "Go on, kiddo, you can go give her a hug. You don't ever have to be afraid to give someone a hug, okay?"

With a slight nod, she slowly rose from the floor. She was like a scared little mouse, and it was breaking my heart. What kind of hell had she lived through in that place to be so scared of everyone?

After lowering onto my knees, I held out my arms for her to come to me. Which she did, she crept slowly up toward me until she stood right up near me, then she wrapped her arms around my neck and buried her face against my throat. Blinking back tears, I wrapped my arms around her little body and rubbed her back gently as I held her, inhaling her sweet smell.

Scout

Watching how Marie was with the little girl was tearing me up inside. She was so fucking good with her. And I'd robbed her of having a baby of her own. Sure, she said she could still technically have a baby, but she wasn't in her twenties any more. Any idiot knew the older a woman got the more risky pregnancy was.

I wanted to kick my own ass for what I'd cost her. And myself. I'd cost us both the joy of having a family by being such a selfish fucking bastard.

Although there was always adoption, and considering Sarah was still in a coma and things weren't looking too good there, this little angel might be looking for a loving home soon. Would that be enough for my Marie? Would raising her sister's child be enough?

Rubbing a palm over my face, I went to adjust my bandana only to find I wasn't wearing one. Fuck. I was so used to having one on, not having one was gonna take some getting used to. But if it meant Marie would have her hands on me more often, I'd deal. Glancing back to her, I could tell she was tired, and the little one was nearly asleep too as Marie continued to tell her tale after tale about her mother as a child and teen. I moved to stand near them.

"Marie? How about we call it a night, love? We can come back first thing in the morning. Maybe by then we'll be able to take the little one to visit her mom, yeah?"

The little girl—dammit, we needed to give her a name—looked up at me bright-eyed. I reached down and stroked her cheek.

"Yeah, that's right. Your mom is very sick, little darlin', but hopefully by morning she'll be well enough we can go see her."

Marie frowned like she was going to argue but Donna cut her off before she could say a word.

"Don't you worry about our little angel. Rose and I have the night shift covered. I got certificated with Child Protection Services years ago to take care of at-risk kids who come into the hospital. You two go home and get a good night's sleep, then you can take over tomorrow and we'll get our rest then."

That reminded me, I needed to call Arrow, see if he'd had any luck seeing that senator yet.

"I'm feeling a little ganged up on right now."

With a chuckle I pressed a kiss to her head. "Yeah, but it's outta love. C'mon, say your goodbyes and we'll be back before you know it."

I stepped back to let the girls have a moment, then smiled when Marie came to me, took my hand and let me lead her out of the hospital. We were halfway to the exit when it occurred to me we had no way to get anywhere.

"Ah, fuck."

"What? What's happened?"

Marie was looking around like she expected someone to jump out at her. I knew better than to tell her how cute she looked doing it.

"I've got no ride here, babe."

"Got that covered, brother." Bulldog came up behind us. "C'mon, I'll get you where you need to go."

"Speaking of rides, don't suppose you know where my phone and keys are?"

"Ah, fuck. Sorry, babe. Forgot all about them."

I reached into my pocket and handed them over to her. Her battery was dead, which she soon figured out. After slipping it into her pocket, she toyed with her keys.

"Has anyone brought my car back yet?"

"Didn't know where it was to collect it, Marie. If you give me your keys and tell me where it is, I'll send a couple of the brothers out to grab it for you."

She handed them over to Bulldog without hesitation. "It's in the parking lot of that little convenience store that was just before the turn off to the compound."

He nodded. "Cool. I'll get it sorted and back to you by morning."

"Thanks."

There was a tiredness to her voice that had me wanting to carry her so she could rest. But I knew she'd see it as me embarrassing her in public, so I beat back the urge. Bulldog pocketed her keys and led us out to his car.

"Any word from Arrow yet?"

"Not yet, prez. I'll let you know the second I hear anything."

The ride back to my place was made in comfortable silence. We were all too damn tired to make conversation. And really, what was there to say? It'd been one hell of a fucked up day. I was also pretty sure Marie would be feeling the same guilt I was about Sarah. Ron had entrusted both Marie and Sarah into my care and when she'd left telling me she just couldn't handle living around bikers, I'd let her go. Biggest fucking mistake of my life. Look where it had landed the poor girl.

After Bulldog pulled up out front of my place, he handed me my keys.

"We found 'em with your cut and other shit. No phone, though. Keys located that off the side of the highway just out of town heading toward Houston. He sent a couple prospects out there, and they found your bike and phone in the bushes. Phone was smashed, and your ride has some damage, but it's nothing you can't fix. It was taken over to the shop."

"Thanks, brother."

With a sigh, I heaved myself out of the car before helping Marie out. I wanted to see how much damage they'd done to my ride, but it could wait. My bike had been my life for so long, but not as much as Marie now was. And I was about to have her in my house. Alone. All to myself. My bike could fucking wait.

My energy level perked up as I thought about everything I wanted to do to her. My inner caveman needed to truly make sure she was doing okay and to make damn sure she knew she'd been claimed by me for good.

Herding her toward the front door, I was vaguely aware of Bulldog pulling out and driving away, but I didn't care. All I wanted right now was Marie. Preferably naked and under me asap.

Rushing to unlock the door, I tapped in the security code, then slammed the door shut and pushed her up against it. Shoving a knee between her thighs, I didn't give her a chance to do more than gasp before my lips were on hers. I held her face between my palms to keep her where I wanted her as I took what was fucking mine.

Her hands wrapped around my wrists as her body relaxed and she began squirming against my thigh. With a growl, I pulled away from her just enough so I could put my shoulder to her middle and lift her over it. She gave a squeal, which I rewarded with a light tap on her ass.

"What the hell do you think you're doing, Scout?"

"Making sure you know who you belong to. You're mine, Marie. Forever."

I gave her ass another slap when she began to slip her fingers inside my jeans. When I got to my room, I slid her down so she was on her feet but didn't waste a second in getting her naked. Her hands were on me too, pulling at my cut and shirt, then my belt. When I got to her jeans, it took way too fucking long to undo the bastards.

"I can see why the other men like their women in short skirts. Could've fucked you up against the door if you'd had one on."

Her own hands fumbled on me as she whimpered, and I grinned like a motherfucker.

"You like that idea, babe? You like the thought that you get me so fucking hard, I want you in a skirt so I can throw you up against a wall and take you whenever the urge strikes?"

I looked into her face as I shoved her jeans over her hips, her pupils had dilated and her mouth was open just a touch as she panted for breath. Oh yeah, she liked that idea a whole lot. Running my gaze down her body, I got even harder thinking about her in a little leather skirt that I could slide up oh so easily so I could get in deep whenever I wanted her.

As she toed off her shoes and got free of her jeans, I did the same. When she stood up straight again, we were both naked. Gripping her hips, I walked her backward until the backs of her legs hit the mattress and she fell onto it. I flowed down onto my knees.

"Lie back, babe. I'm gonna get me a taste of this sweet pussy."

Her body trembled and with wide eyes, she slowly lay back on the mattress. I loved how her tits settled into place, their nipples tight and hard little points waiting for some love. I'd get there, but first... With a palm on each knee, I spread her legs to give myself some room. Kissing her inner knee, I made my way slowly closer. She was strung so tight, I wanted her to relax a little. Fuck, I needed her to enjoy this.

My glaze lowered to her pussy and my heart skipped a beat. Fuck me. Her neatly trimmed curls were the sexiest thing I'd seen in a long time. I'd only gotten a glimpse at the hotel. All the club whores were bare, but my Marie was natural, and so fucking beautiful. And she was wet for me, little droplets of her moisture clinging to her curls.

"So fucking gorgeous, babe. I've got a feeling I'm gonna spend a lot of time in the future eating you up."

"Stop teasing me already, Charlie!"

I nipped her inner thigh lightly, before rubbing my beard over her sensitive skin. Then, using my thumbs, I held her pussy lips open and blew a breath over her core before I delved my tongue in deep, getting a good mouthful of her cream before I swallowed it down.

"Hmmm. As sweet as the rest of you, just like I knew it would be."

Chapter 8

Marie

Oral sex wasn't something I'd ever experienced. My only attempt at sex prior to Scout was a crazy, rushed fumble in the back of a car when I was seventeen. But this, oh my goodness, this was heaven and bliss and all things wonderful. I gripped tight handfuls of the sheets as my back arched up while Scout made a meal out of me. He hummed and growled as he licked and nipped. Each time he delved that talented tongue of his into my core, I clenched down on it, trying to hold it within me.

"Charlie, please!"

He was driving me insane.

"Let go, Marie. Come for me. I need the taste of your climax down my throat."

He'd barely lifted his mouth from my flesh to speak so the vibrations from his voice, together with the words themselves had me flying higher. Then he moved and blew my world wide open. He pinched my clit at the same time he thrust his tongue in deep and with a scream, I was sailing high.

I had no idea how long I was lost to the waves of intense pleasure that were flowing through me, but when I blinked open my eyes next, Scout had shifted me fully on the bed and was kneeling between my thighs, slowly stroking his very erect dick with his large palm. My gaze was drawn to the sight, like it was calling me and I licked my lips. He groaned and gripped himself tighter.

"I would love nothing more than to feel your mouth on me, babe. But not right now. I need to be inside you so fucking bad, I can't think straight. Can I take you bare? I promise I'm clean. Never fucked without wrapping it up before."

I nodded before I could analyze that statement too much. I didn't want his past sex life to ruin this moment.

"Take me, Charlie. Make me yours."

He grinned with a little shake of his head at my use of his birth name. Then he dropped over me, a hand on either side of my head holding his weight off me. He smelled like me, and I realized my cream was all through his beard. Before I could say anything about it, his lips were on mine. I could taste myself on his tongue and it sent an erotic shiver through me. He continued to kiss me as he shifted his weight to one arm while he used the other to grip my thigh to move it out as he thrust his hips forward. I gasped into the kiss, wrapping my fingers around his solid shoulders, as he impaled me completely on that first stroke. With a growl, he broke the kiss to trail his lips all over my face. I moved my hips with him, arching up so he could get deeper inside me, where I needed him. My heart was pounding so hard, I could hear it in my ears. When he pulled his face from my throat, I held his gaze with mine and poured all my love into my gaze. Did I dare say the words out loud? Would he run if I did?

A groan tore from me when on each in stroke he twisted his hips so he ground against my clit. He rested his forehead against mine as he sped up his movements, taking me higher and higher yet again.

Then just as I was about to fly over the edge for a second time, an image of Scout hung in that room, injured and hurting, flashed across my mind that left me crying out. Pain and pleasure mixed inside me into a storm I had no hope of controlling as everything crashed around me. The orgasm was powerful and my body shook from the force of it, while my heart ached at the thought I could have lost him today. That this night nearly didn't happen.

I slid my arms as far around his shoulders as I could reach, holding him tightly to me as I sobbed into his chest.

"Hey, whoa. Sweetheart, did I hurt you? *Fuck.*"

Scout rolled us so I was on top of him, his dick slipping from my body with a slight rush of liquid, which left me crying harder. We'd just shared something beautiful, sexy as hell but still beautiful, and I was ruining it all with my emotions.

"Not hurt."

His body relaxed a little and he began to stroke my hair and back with his big palms and callused fingers.

"Thank fuck. That was intense, huh?"

He didn't say anything else, just kept up with the soothing back rub until I calmed enough to be able to speak.

"I thought he was going to kill you." *Hiccup.* "I thought I was going to lose you." *Hiccup.* "Before I even really had you."

He wrapped his arms around me and held me tightly against him.

"Funny, I thought the same fucking thing when you walked in that damn room. Why the hell did you come on your own, babe? You had to have known the MC would have had your back."

"There wasn't time. Sarah came into the cafe saying you'd already been there for hours. That they'd already hurt you. I didn't have time to call anyone, and Sarah told me if the whole club stormed the place, they'd kill you and run. I couldn't risk that. And Zara was there, she was eavesdropping and I gave her a nod when she held up her phone, out of Sarah's view. I knew she'd call Mac and that Keys could trace my phone to follow us."

That got me a growl. "Fuck, babe. Never again, you hear me? Shit like this goes down ever again, you go straight to the club. You call Bulldog or, hell, any of the other patched in brothers and you do what you're fucking told. You're my heart, Marie. Without you I'm dead anyway. You're not allowed to fucking risk yourself like that."

I pushed myself up, his grip loosening to allow me to move a little. I stared straight into his clear blue irises, making sure he knew I meant business.

"You don't think I feel the same way about you? Hell, Scout, I've loved you for over twenty damn years! You don't think that just the thought of you gone from my life is enough to cripple me?"

He gently stroked his fingers over my face, wiping away the few tears that had continued to flow.

"So why'd you run from the hotel?"

"Because I was scared you'd be done with me after my meltdown. I yelled at you, said things..."

He stopped me talking with a light kiss.

"Babe, you yelling at me ain't gonna send me packing. I was being a fucking dickhead caveman. I deserved to be yelled at. And you're right. I've cost you so fucking much. Never intended to, but I have. I can't apologize enough for being such a damn fool for so long. But that's over now. I'm serious, Marie. You're mine. I'm gonna order your cut tomorrow. You're my old lady, you'll wear my patch and we'll build our own family. If it's too late for us to have a baby of our own, we'll adopt or something. I will give you a family, Marie. I promise."

Warmth bloomed in my heart and spread over my body. I couldn't find words so I lowered my face to his, gently kissing his lips. More tears filled my eyes. Why couldn't we have done this twenty years ago? With a growl, Scout took control of the kiss, rolling us over so I was beneath him once more. Using a knee he spread my thighs and a moment later, he slid his thick erection deep within me again. I groaned and arched at how good it felt to be filled with him.

"That's some recovery time. Thought you old men needed time between rounds."

"If I could reach your ass, I'd spank it for that comment, woman. There ain't nothing wrong with my recovery time when I got you anywhere near me, and you know it."

I decided right then and there, I was through with looking back and focusing on regrets. Scout was right. We'd move forward together and make our own family. Somehow.

"I love you, Charlie Dalton."

On his next thrust in, he held still a moment and grinned down at me. "And I love you Marie Parker-soon-to-be-Dalton."

I was about to throw back some more cheek but he got serious about making love and all my thoughts whirled together, then left me. Especially when he slipped a palm behind my back and lifted my chest so he could suckle on my nipples as he continued to thrust into my core.

I could get very used to this treatment.

Scout

Waking up to Marie nestled in beside me was hands down the best way to wake up. Careful not to disturb her, I shifted to tilt my head so I could watch her. I was flat on my back with her up against my side, tucked under my arm. Her pale hand was resting on my right pec, while her head was nestled in against the hollow of my shoulder. One of her nipples was peeking out from where her breast was pressed up to my side, and I barely resisted the urge to tweak the tempting little bud.

The sheets I'd pulled over us after I'd taken her for the second time last night had worked their way down to our waists. But despite our legs being covered, I knew she had one slung over mine, with her hot pussy pressed against my hip. Basically, she was a soft, sexy bundle of femininity and I was never going to get enough of her. A quick glance at my alarm clock told me it was time we got up and got moving, but I needed something first. One more taste of her before we got caught up in the drama today would bring. And I was certain there would be drama. Between Sarah being in a coma and the issues surrounding her daughter, there was no question our day was gonna go downhill fast once we left the house.

However, I was sure between lovin' on my woman this morning, and working over the fucker I had waiting for me in the clubhouse basement later, I'd be able to get through whatever the day brought with it.

With gentle fingers, I brushed the hair from her face and tucked it behind her ear.

"Hey, love, time to wake up."

I grinned when, with a moan, she rubbed her face against me. She was so fucking adorable. Then she wriggled her pussy against my thigh and that was it. With a growl, I pulled her fully on top of me, so the length of my cock was pressed against her wet pussy. She arched and squirmed against me for a minute before she pressed her palms against my pecs and lifted herself up to kneel over me. Her nipples were hard little buds and I couldn't resist, especially when she lifted her arms above her head to stretch out her back and they thrust further forward.

Sitting up, I slid one palm up the smooth silky skin of her back to hold her in position while I wrapped my mouth over one of her tight little buds. I ran my other palm up her torso until I had her other breast in my palm, then I started to knead the flesh as I nipped and suckled at the one in my mouth. She tasted so fucking good. As I moved to get my mouth to the other side, she threaded her fingers through my hair, tugging a little when I bit down on her flesh. When she scraped her finger nails over my scalp, a shiver ran down my spine and I decided I could live without my bandana if this was the reward. It was gonna take me some time to not reach for it during the day, I'd been wearing one for decades and readjusting the damn thing was like a nervous twitch I couldn't help. But the feeling of what she just did was so much better.

Releasing her flesh with a pop, I gripped her hips to lift her so I could impale her on my cock but she clenched her knees, holding herself up. I raised an eyebrow in question.

"You sick of me already, babe?"

A sweet fucking blush reddened her cheeks. "No, of course not. But before the other night at the hotel? I hadn't had sex for twenty-six years, Scout. I'm sore."

I winced. Yeah, I'd done that too. Forced that fucking long dry spell on her. And I bet she was sore. Dammit. Then another idea struck me and I grinned at her.

"Not sure I like that grin you're wearing."

"Oh, you will. Shower time."

She gently rested her palm over the bandage over my ribs.

"What about your stitches?"

"Waterproof dressing, babe. I'll just take off the bandage, then I'm good to go."

With a chuckle, she leaned down and ran her fingernails over my head one more time before she swung her leg over me and left the bed. She was halfway to the bathroom when she stopped to look over her shoulder.

"You coming, or what?"

I rolled out bed, never taking my gaze off her sexy body.

"Wouldn't want you to have to wash your own back now, would we?"

Before she turned her face away, I caught the grin she wore. This playful Marie was a new side I'd not seen before but I liked it. Actually, I fucking loved it. Following her into my bathroom, I unwrapped the bandage and double checked the waterproof dressing was securely affixed to my skin around the stitches before I tossed the bandage in the trash and refocused on Marie. She was leaning into the shower, twisting the taps on. My gaze got caught on her ass. Damn, but she was so fucking gorgeous. Not stick thin like most of the club whores, nope, my woman had curves and a little padding I fucking adored.

I moved in close behind her and ran my palms over the curve of her hips and waist as I pressed my hard cock against the crease of her ass. My groan echoed off the tiles when she wriggled her hips and chuckled. As she stepped away from me and under the spray, she turned to face me. The water flattened her hair and flowed down her body, dripping from her hard little nipples, getting caught in the dark curls that covered her pussy. I stepped into the stall and slid the door shut as I wrapped a hand around my cock to give it a few strokes. The old boy didn't give a fuck she was sore, he wanted in, and he wanted in *now*.

"Got a problem there, Charlie?"

Fuck, I loved how she said my birth name. No one had used it in so long, which had never bothered me because I never cared for it. But from her lips? Fucking loved it. She didn't give me a chance to respond before she was gripping my hips and lowering herself down onto the tiles.

"I've never done this before..."

She was gonna kill me. "You'll do perfect, babe. Just follow your instincts."

Part of me wanted to order her to do exactly what I wanted her to do, but the fact this was the first time she'd given a blow job, together with the fact she'd instigated this, meant I was content to let her take the lead and play as she wished this time. Well, at least for now, anyhow. I wasn't sure how long I could play the indulgent lover before my inner caveman came back out.

All my thoughts emptied out of my mind as I hissed out my breath when she began to tentatively explore my length with first her fingers, then her mouth. Gentle little kisses and licks that were driving me fucking insane. I was about to say fuck it and grab a fist full of her hair to guide her when she took the head of my cock into her mouth and sucked.

"Fuck!"

I'd received hundreds, maybe thousands of blow jobs over the years, but this? Marie on her knees in front of me with her mouth full of my cock and a sparkle in her eye? This was fucking heaven and blew away any memory I had of any other woman. I would never give this up, give *her* up. I knew in that moment that I'd do whatever the fuck I needed to in order keep this woman happy, safe and by my side.

It didn't take long before a tingle ran down my spine and landed in my balls. When they drew up ready to blow, I stroked her cheek to get her attention.

"I'm gonna come, babe. If you don't want to swallow, you need to stop now."

Without releasing me, she shook her head, the sensation making me groan again. Then she took me deeper in her mouth and lifted her palm to cup and stroke my balls. That's all it took and I was gone. Delving my fingers into her hair, trying to keep it loose enough so she could pull away if she needed to, I held her as I pumped into her mouth until I came. Her throat moved as she swallowed but there was too much for her, and two little white trails leaked down from the edges of her lips that were stretched around my dick. The sight had my cock twitching, wanting more. But that wasn't gonna happen right now. Pulling free from her mouth, I reached down and helped her to stand then moved her under the spray. It killed me to see my seed get washed off her, but knowing I'd filled up her pussy twice last night on top of what she'd just swallowed down, helped ease the need to have her marked as mine.

We stayed silent as I slowly, carefully, washed her from head to toe. It was a comfortable quiet, with just the water hitting the tiles and our breathing filling the air. After I took some extra time to make sure her tits and pussy were *very* clean, she took the cloth from me and returned the favor, leaving me hard and ready to go again. Damn, I hadn't been this fucking insatiable since I was in my early twenties.

She wrapped her hand around my length and started stroking me.

"Babe, as great as that feels, we really should get moving. Got a shit load to do today."

As though reality had just crashed down on her, Marie gasped and jumped back from me, nearly slipping on the wet tile. I reached for her and pulled her back against me before she hurt herself.

"Shh, Marie. We're good. It's perfectly okay to take some time out for yourself. Both Sarah and her daughter are in good hands, getting everything they need medically."

She shook her head and tears filled her eyes, which gutted me all over again. I fucking hated seeing her cry.

"I can't believe I forgot about them. What kind of monster does that make me?"

I cupped her face and tilted it up so I could stare straight into her eyes.

"It makes you human. I made you wait over twenty years for last night and this morning, don't let outside factors ruin it. We had an extremely long-overdue beautiful, glorious night of passion. Now, we'll get dressed and deal with all the other shit going on out there before we come back here again tonight and repeat last night. That's how this is going to go. The real world can have us during the day, but after all that shit is done, once it's just the two of us alone? Then it's gonna be all about us, baby."

I didn't give her time to speak, instead sealed my words with a kiss as I reached behind her to flip off the taps. Taking her hand I led her out of the stall and grabbing a towel, I dried her off first, then myself. By the time I got to the bedroom, Marie was going through the bag Bulldog had brought to the hospital for her.

"We'll head to your place today for you grab some more stuff, 'kay?"

She nodded as she got dressed, but clearly she'd gone from my soft, teasing lover to the concerned sister and aunt.

"You wanna eat here or grab something at the hospital?"

She glanced at the clock and gasped at the time.

"No time to eat. We should have been at the hospital an hour ago."

I didn't bother trying to calm her down this time. It was now past ten am, so she had a point. We were late. I quickly dressed and snatched up my phone and keys and followed her, trying not to chuckle, as she raced toward the front of the house like a kid about to miss the school bus.

Fifteen minutes later we arrived at the hospital. Marie wanted to go straight to Sarah's daughter's room. We really needed to give that kid a name. "Sarah's daughter" was too fucking long to keep saying. But I convinced her to stop at the reception desk to see if we could see Sarah's doctor first. Once I suggested it, Marie was all for it, and looked a little guilty over not wanting to do that in the first place. Her big heart was one of the many reasons I loved this woman, but I hated when it caused her to beat herself up like she was at the moment.

It took a little doing, but we finally got to talk with Sarah's doctor. After he shook both our hands, he wasted no time explaining the situation.

"We've done all we can for now. She's in a coma, but is stable. Physically, she will recover. There are no breaks to any of her vertebra or damage to her spinal cord. She has bruising to around sixty percent of her body and the concussion isn't helping things. We're concerned she's not waking due to the swelling of her brain. We've started her on Dexamethasone to reduce that and hopefully that will have her waking up soon. We can't know what damage will be left behind until she wakes, if she wakes. At this point, we just need to wait for the drugs to do their thing. Hopefully her will to live is strong and that'll help speed things along."

Marie caught her sob with a hand over mouth, and I pulled her in against me to hold her while she regrouped.

"Doc, we were thinking of taking her daughter up to see her today. You think that'll be a good idea?"

The doc was silent for a few moments.

"Hearing her voice might be what it takes to pull Sarah out of her coma." He paused and with a frown, shook his head. "I forgot the child is mute. Still, maybe her touch will remind Sarah what she has to live for and help bring her around. But if the child shows any sign of distress, she needs to be removed immediately. That girl has a hard enough road ahead of her as it is, we don't need to go adding to it."

"Of course. First sign of distress, we'll have her out of there in a flash."

After saying goodbye and the doc promising to come up to see Sarah later, hopefully while we had her daughter there, I guided Marie to the child's room. Silently praying the whole time we didn't do more damage to the poor kid by taking her to see her mom.

Chapter 9

Sarah

Images and sounds all jumbled together and floated around my mind. I couldn't quite grab hold of any one thing, but it wasn't so bad. My body was light, so light. And there was no pain. I didn't feel happy, but I wasn't sad either. It was a strange sensation, this floating in nothingness. With nothing to worry about, I could stay here forever.

Then a scent flowed through the mix and things grew more defined. Images of me pushing out my baby girl. Being so scared because Bruce refused to take me to the hospital. But my little angel had made it safely into the world. She was so beautiful. My little Ariel. I hoped she'd break free from our prison to live her life like the little mermaid had. Bruce had been so mad that I'd gotten pregnant, even though he was the one who had refused to replace my birth control. My nights had been nothing but a blur for so long, I never remembered them, but Ariel was proof of what must happen.

Another breath in and more of her scent filled me. She needed me, Ariel needed her mommy. I fought to swim through the mess of my mind to find a way out, to get to my little girl. To find out if we were safe. Was this some new trickery that Bruce was pulling on me? The next images that flashed through my mind were of me, digging the knife I kept in my boot deep into his gut. Had I killed him? The image went black after that and before I could try to grab it again, a small voice whispered to me.

"Momma, safe now. Wake up."

God, her whisper-quiet voice. Ariel had never spoken to anyone other than me. Bruce had made it clear from the very start that "the kid" was to not only be not seen, but not heard, either. My poor little girl had been forced to learn so much in her short life. I'd done my best to save her enough food from meal times, two of the men helped too, smuggling in tins of formula and bottles when she'd been a baby. But it wasn't enough. She was so tiny. She was four years old but looked only about two. My eyes stung with tears. Pain roared up my spine and over my head as I broke through the last of the fog to find my way to my daughter who was pressed up against my left side, her little hand over my heart.

"Baby."

A feminine gasp, followed by a sob and male cursing followed my single word. I tried to wrap my arm tighter around Ariel, to protect her from whoever was with us. But I couldn't be sure I'd managed the move. Holding my breath and focusing the little bit of energy I had, I forced my eyelids to open. The bright light stung so bad that I slammed them shut right away.

"Someone turn down the lights!"

I knew that voice, from long ago. Who was she... Marie! My foster sister. That's right. Warmth surrounded my right hand and I knew it was she who had picked up my hand. If only I'd stayed with her.

"C'mon, Sarah. Come back to us."

I tried again to blink open my eyes, this time keeping them open as the bright, white light had been dimmed. I turned my gaze to the left, my head was too heavy to move, but my eyes could move enough that I could see my little girl.

"Ariel, my sweet girl. You be good for Marie, okay? We can trust her and Scout."

"Yes, Momma."

"Oh, my—she can speak!"

Marie's words cracked my heart. My poor baby must have been so scared. I turned my gaze to Marie.

"Bruce? Is he?"

"He's dead. The compound was cleaned out and blown up. You're both safe."

Deep down I knew my mind wasn't going to allow me to enjoy that safety. I was already struggling to hold on to reality. Memories and thoughts were fading and coming back, but altering slightly each time. I couldn't move my body, as though I was paralyzed, but I could feel so I mustn't be. I could easily feel the warmth of Marie's hands, the heat of Ariel's little body against me.

"There's a book in my room at the compound. About Ariel. Find the book." Then I looked back to Ariel.

"Baby, you hear that? You're safe. You can talk as loud as you like, to whoever you like. You stay with Marie and Scout. That was my mistake. I left. I'm sorry, Ariel, so very sorry. Love you, baby."

Then my time was up, and as though I'd been sucked down a deep dark hole, I was jerked away from reality and back to the emptiness inside me. What had seemed so peaceful and nice earlier was dark and hollow now. I wanted to see my baby again. Wanted to hold her, read her a story, take her to the park... all the normal things I'd never been able to do with her. I wanted to catch all the memories I could only see glimpses of. Her birth, first steps, the first whispered words.

It wasn't fair! I wanted to scream, to throw things. But I couldn't do a damn thing. Then suddenly, dark black liquid began to rise up around me. It rose fast, soon I was treading water to keep my head above it, but then I couldn't kick anymore. Something wrapped around my ankles and pulled me under and with a silent scream, my mouth and lungs filled with the blackness and I choked as I was pulled further down, further away from my life, my daughter. I knew when my heart was about to beat its last beat, knew this was the end and I prayed Marie would take care of Ariel better than I had. That my girl would have a good, happy life with Marie as her mother.

Marie

I could barely process the last few minutes. Had any of it been real?

Sarah had woken.

Her daughter had spoken.

One of the positives was Sarah calling her daughter Ariel so we finally had a name for the little girl. Then, just when I was getting my hopes up that Sarah was going to be okay, her eyes shut and she went limp against the bed. The hand I held between mine was lifeless. I moved my fingers, searching for a pulse until I found it, refusing to give up this time. I'd found it, but it was incredibly weak. Suddenly, Sarah's whole body went tense, her back arched up and her mouth opened in a silent scream. Ariel began to silently sob and shake. Scout had been standing near her, and he quickly gathered her up off the bed and rushed out the door, getting the little girl away from whatever was going on here. I knew I should go too, but I couldn't move. Frozen to the spot, I watched as her doctor raced to her side just as Sarah suddenly began to struggle to breathe. Machines began to make all sorts of horrid noises and nurses came running into the room, yet still I couldn't move, even though I knew on some level I was in the way and not helping anything by staying. Why couldn't she breathe? She was fine a minute ago. When I was scooped up I jolted from my stupor to look up at Bulldog's stoic face.

He'd gathered me up like Scout had Ariel and was heading toward the door.

"No! I can't leave her!"

I looked back toward Sarah—the doctor had paddles on her chest, shocking her—trying to bring her back, but it wasn't working. The machines still screamed. Then a nurse flipped a few switches and in the new silence, I heard the doctor call her time of death.

"Noooo!"

"She's not there anymore, darlin'. She's gone. Bruce's drugs fucked her up too badly, the concussion made it worse. She tried, we all saw her try to come back."

With a wail I clung to him and sobbed. My sister, she was gone? For real this time. I was unaware we were moving until I was laid on a hospital bed. I was crying so hard, I could barely see. Not that I wanted to. My grief was too strong. Then a tiny little hand touched my face. I blinked clear my eyes until I could see a watery vision of Sarah's daughter. Ariel.

"Oh, baby. I'm so sorry, sweetheart."

I held out an arm, and the little girl crawled in next to me and buried her face in against my breasts before her whole body trembled with her own grief.

"Let it out, Ariel. You cry, scream, yell, whatever you need to do. You go right ahead, sweetheart. I've got you."

I looked up over her to see Scout, Bulldog, Rose and Donna all standing in the room. All with red eyes, and all swiping at tears. I focused on Scout. How had this day gone from heaven to hell so fast? I was really over this roller coaster my life had become recently.

Holding my gaze, Scout came to me. Leaning down he pressed a soft kiss to my lips before he stroked a hand over Ariel's head. Then, he moved to sit in the seat beside the bed and kept a palm stroking either my hair or Ariel's, until my tears ran out and Ariel had fallen asleep.

I locked my gaze with Scout's before I spoke in a quiet voice.

"Did anyone gather up anything before you destroyed that place?"

Scout turned from me to Bulldog, who cleared his throat before he spoke.

"Yeah, we did a fast but thorough search of the place. When a couple of the brothers found what looked like Sarah and Ariel's room they grabbed boxes and shoved everything they could into them. They're safe back at the clubhouse."

"I need to find that book, see what she wrote in there about Ariel." I looked back to Scout. "Do you think they'll let us keep her?"

The thought of Ariel ending up in the system was enough to make my heart bleed. I was lucky, I got good foster parents first off, but I knew so many others that weren't so lucky. Ariel had been through enough already. She didn't need more drama.

"I've already got Arrow working on getting us listed as her foster parents. I'll call him in a bit and get him to change things from foster to adoption, if he can."

That had me frowning. "Don't we have to petition the court and pass tests and stuff?"

"Normally, yeah, but I'm calling in some markers to get this done fast."

I didn't ask anything else, knowing I didn't want to know anything to do with club business. So long as I got to have Ariel to raise and protect, to love, I'd be happy.

"But even if what Arrow is doing fails, I promise you this, Marie. I will move heaven and earth if I have to so Ariel can stay with us. I fucking failed Sarah so badly, I refuse to ever fail her daughter in any way."

I knew if we weren't careful, the guilt over Sarah was going to eat us both up. Considering how much I was struggling, I could only imagine how Scout was feeling.

"She made her choice. I tried everything I could to get her to stay, but after what happened she wanted to be far away from all things biker. Guess she'd never considered there were people out there more evil than the Hammers."

I stroked Ariel's soft hair. Even after telling her to let it out, she'd cried silently until she fell asleep against me. What had happened in that place to make such a small child so quiet? Would she talk to me now that Sarah had told her it was okay? I hoped so.

Bulldog cleared his throat again. "Prez, we need to head over to the clubhouse to handle a few things. I'll help you look through those boxes while we're there. I've got Jazz and Keg out in the hall to keep the girls protected."

Scout nodded absently, like he knew he had to go but didn't want to.

"Yeah, I know. I'm sorry, Marie. I'm gonna have to leave you for a bit. I'll get that book for you and be back in a few hours. Okay?"

I gave him a nod.

"I know how much work being president is, Scout. Go do your thing. I'm just gonna have a little rest here with Ariel while you're gone. I'm so damn tired."

He leaned over and pressed another soft kiss on my lips. "If I get time I'll swing by the cafe and see how the girls are holding up."

"Thanks."

As I watched him walk out, my thoughts turned to my business. If we did get Ariel, what would happen to my cafe? At least for now Ariel needed someone with her full-time who she could learn to trust. I needed to find more staff. Zara was great, and Mercedes was showing potential, but I was going to need more than two employees if I wasn't going to be working every day myself.

Donna and Rose came to sit closer to the bed.

"You let us know anything we can do to help, Marie. We're all here for you and little Ariel."

I looked into both their faces. I'd known these women for so long now. I might not have officially been Scout's old lady, but the women of the club had always treated me like I was one of their own. I realized it wasn't just for Scout that I'd stayed in Bridgewater all these years. No, it was for these women and the way they stuck together, too. The Charon MC really was a family.

"I'm going to need to find more help at the cafe. Ariel's gonna need me twenty-four/seven for a while, I suspect."

The both nodded. Rose speaking up. "I'll talk to Zara about it, see if she's noticed anyone coming in who might be a good fit."

"That would be great. Thank you."

Donna tapped a finger against her lips. "You know what business the Charons need to open next? A child care center. Silk and Zara have both had babies, Flick isn't far off delivering her little bundle. Add in Ariel here, we're gonna need somewhere we can trust to look after all our kiddos so the mommas can work and catch a break."

Rose's eyes lit up as she turned to Donna. "Oh, I would love to head up that project." She turned back toward me. "You see, I used to work in a kindergarten before I retired. I'd happily manage a child care center. And I'd get more time with my little grandson. Raven's just so damn adorable."

I couldn't help but smile at the two women as they started planning between themselves. Eventually, I cut into the conversation.

"I think that sounds great, but I suspect Ariel's never even seen another child before. I'm not sure how long it's going to take to help her adjust socially."

"Oh, this project won't happen overnight. This'll take time to get the permits and sort out a building, find staff. We'll have plenty of time to help little Ariel find her feet in the world."

Tears sprung from my eyes again.

"Thank you both. Thank you so much. For everything."

"Oh, sweetheart, no need to thank us. We're family, and this Charon MC family always, *always* takes care of its own."

I gave them a watery smile, then let my tired eyelids close as they continued to discuss child care center plans. Maybe, just maybe, this would all work out after all. Even if Sarah dying had left a hole in my heart and soul that I wasn't sure I'd ever be able to fix.

Chapter 10

Scout

Before we got out of the hospital Donald grabbed us and ushered us into an empty room, where he shut the door. Donald was our main contact with the police here in town and we helped each other out if we could.

"I understand Sarah passed away this morning."

"Yeah, she did. The doctor said something about a brain bleed, but I guess we won't know for sure until they conduct the autopsy."

I'd given him a statement while Marie had still been sleeping off what Donna had given her, so I didn't need to recap everything that had gone on at the ranch house.

"With the way that place blew up, there was no evidence. We've had to let the three men go without charging them."

He was glaring at me because he knew full well the Charons were behind the explosion and the bodies found inside the house. I ignored his stare.

"When did you release them?"

I didn't think they'd be dumb enough to come after me again, not after what they saw happen and what my brothers would have threatened them with, but you never knew. Some people were fucking morons.

"Not long ago. Two of the men were very concerned for Sarah, kept asking if she and the kid were okay. The third guy was in a helluva mood. He's the one I'd be watching out for if I were you."

"Can you give me a name?"

"You know I can't, but I can tell you it was the youngest of the three. Now, if you'll excuse me, I need to go talk to the doctor. Maybe we can find something to use to charge those three with something over all this shit after all."

For a moment I thought about telling him about the book, but in the end decided against it. If the book revealed those three were guilty of something, we'd take care of it—Charon style.

We followed Donald out of the room and when he turned to head deeper into the hospital, I headed to the front door with Bulldog, groaning when I got to my ride. I was still stuck driving my damn cage, and had no fucking clue when I'd be able to get to the shop to check out the damage to my bike. As I made my way to the clubhouse, with Bulldog riding behind me, I figured I may as well get used to the cage. If we ended up with Ariel, we'd have to take a cage most places from now on, anyhow.

I was relieved to see the parking lot was nearly empty when I pulled in. It meant I wasn't going to be hounded with questions while I was here. I quickly got out and headed to the front entrance where the prospect at the door gave me a head tilt as I passed by and entered the building. Knowing Bulldog was following me, I headed directly to my office. As soon as I entered, I noticed a few boxes in the corner.

"I got the boys to stick Sarah's stuff in here to keep it safe until we figured out what the hell we're gonna do with it all."

Walking over to them, I flipped open the flap of the top one to look inside. Not much, some worn looking clothing, and a ragged looking rabbit.

"After we go through and find that diary of Sarah's, we'll sort it out and store it for Ariel." I lifted out the rabbit. "Except for the stuff that's obviously Ariel's. I'll take this to her when we head back later."

Silence filled the room for a minute.

"That poor fucking kid. What the fuck makes a toddler be so quiet? I've never seen a little girl that hasn't chattered all day, every day."

"We've only been around happy, well cared for kiddos, brother. I suspect that diary is going to be one fucking hard book to read."

Bulldog came to stand next to me and rested a palm on my shoulder. "We got that fucker downstairs to deal with too. You want me to get Taz to take care of him for you? Let you get back to Marie and Ariel faster? I know as president you want to lead the charge in teaching him a lesson, but you gotta get your priorities straight here. If you're really stepping up to claim Marie, and, in turn, Ariel, they gotta come first. Let your brothers help you out. You've seen what Taz can do, you know he'll make that fucker suffer before he's allowed to die."

I nodded as I huffed out a breath. I had so much to do, and Bulldog was right, I needed to utilize my brothers, let them help me.

"I'll do down there first, do a little damage then leave him for Taz to finish off. I need to do that much. Then, I'll come sort these boxes out. Don't suppose you feel like helping me out with that?"

He squeezed my shoulder a second before releasing it. "Sure thing, brother. Anything else that needs doing?"

"Yeah, I need to order Marie her cut. Can you put it through for me? Make it a rush job?"

That had the other man grinning. "Sure thing, prez. Be my pleasure. Should have it by the weekend, if you want to have a family BBQ. It can be a welcome for Ariel, too."

A warmth filled my heart at the thought. "Not sure she'll be up for that just yet. We'll make it about Marie, let Ariel get used to us all slowly. I'm pretty sure that little girl has never been the center of anyone's attention—well, aside from Sarah that is. Call church for this afternoon. Let me know the time, I'll do my best to get back here. If not, you know what needs to be said."

Bulldog's smile dimmed some. "Sure. And sorry, I hadn't thought about that side of what Ariel's been through. Right, so you go do your thing down in the basement, I'll start making calls. Then we'll get these boxes sorted out so you can get back to your woman."

With a nod, I left Bulldog in my office and headed toward the back of the building, where the hidden stairs were. With a roll of my shoulders I headed down to the cells, to where the fucker who'd cut me up was waiting for me. Bank was standing beside the door, keeping guard. When he saw me he turned and unlocked the door for me. I flipped on the light before I stepped inside the bare concrete room.

"Quiet fucker. Barely made a noise all night."

I nodded. "Lucky for you. Screamers are the fucking worst."

"True that, prez. You need a hand with him?"

"Nah, I'm gonna have my fun then leave him for Taz to finish off. You can stay if you want to."

The bastard had both his ankles and wrists shackled to the wall and his head hung down like he was fucking asleep. I was a little insulted he was so fucking relaxed. The table against the other wall held all sorts of fun toys, and a bucket of water. Which I knew was gonna feel like ice against his skin. It was fucking cold down here in the basement.

Lifting the bucket, I tossed the contents at him, standing back so I didn't get any of it on me while he sputtered and coughed. After shaking the water from his face, he silently glared at me as though he could intimidate me.

"Morning, sleeping beauty. Remember me?"

When he just sneered, I had to chuckle. "Still playing the tough guy, huh? That's okay. I can deal with that."

I went and picked up the largest knife from the table and strode right up to stand before him. His eyes went wide and some of the color drained from his face. *Well, that was a little too easy.* Holding the bottom of his shirt, I sliced it up the middle before tearing it off his body completely.

"You help that fucker make those drugs of his?"

His head shook as his gaze stayed glued to the blade in my hand.

"No? Yeah, you ain't that fucking clever, are you? But I bet you made the most of Sarah when she was high on that shit, though."

"No man could resist Sarah after she'd had a hit. She was all over any man she came across till she got cock. Not my fault."

I slashed the first cut along his ribs, just like he'd done to me yesterday. Unlike me, he didn't suffer silently. Nope, fucker squealed like a pig.

"Bull-fucking-shit. You could have locked her in her room or somewhere else safe, until the effects wore off. Hell, you could have been a real fucking man and got her the hell out of there when you realized what was being done to her. You didn't have to rape her."

"It wasn't like that! She wanted it. No one raped her!"

"She was given drugs without her knowledge, drugs that altered her state of mind. Did Sarah ever go looking for sex when she wasn't high? Yeah, didn't think so."

I made another slice. He'd given me four of the fucking things, the least I could do was return the favor.

"But then you made the biggest fucking mistake by helping that motherfucker take me. How the fuck did you think kidnapping the president of an MC was gonna end?"

He groaned and licked his lips before he responded. "Bruce told us we'd get a cut of the profits from whatever ya'll are running out of that bunker of his daddy's."

"And you fell for that shit? Seriously, how fucking stupid are you? If that's what he really wanted out of this situation, he wouldn't have taken me. Or at least if he did take me, he wouldn't have fucking had me tortured. He was after Sarah's foster sister. You're gonna die because Bruce wanted revenge for something those two didn't even fucking do twenty-five fucking years ago."

I made quick work of giving him the last two slices, waiting for his screams to die down before I spoke again.

"Now, I've repaid you what you did to me. I gotta go deal with more important things than your sorry ass, but don't worry. You won't be alone for long. One of my brothers, who was a Marine for years, has all sorts of things he wants to practice with you. So, have fun with that. And enjoy hell, you piece of shit."

I landed my fist against his jaw hard enough to knock the asshole out, before I turned, dumped the knife on the table and headed out the door. I washed my hands before I left the basement, then went straight to my office where I found Bulldog lowering his phone from his ear.

"Perfect timing, prez. All sorted for church today at five-thirty. We'll have a few missing, but I'll catch them later and let them know what they need to."

I gave him a nod. "Right. Well, let's get these boxes sorted."

Marie

The press of lips along with the tickle of a beard against my forehead woke me from my sleep with a smile.

"Hmmm, hey, Scout."

I tilted up my head and he kissed my mouth, slow and gentle, before he pulled back and glanced down at the bundle beginning to stir against me. Ariel pressed closer to me for a moment before she jerked back with wide eyes.

"Shhh, sugar. You're okay."

Her eyes welled with tears, and I guessed she was remembering what happened before she fell asleep.

"Ariel? I found some of your things earlier. I thought you might like to have them."

Her gaze flicked over to Scout, who was holding up a dirty, ratty looking plush rabbit. Her face lit up and she reached a hand for the toy. Scout handed it over then ran his hand over her head as she hugged the rabbit tightly and relaxed back down on the mattress next to me with a small sigh.

"Thank you for bringing it. I had no idea she even had any toys, let alone a favorite one. What else did you find?"

His expression turned serious. "The men grabbed everything from their room by the looks of it. Some old clothes, a couple toys, basic toiletries. And Sarah's diary. I haven't read it all, I just skimmed through looking for details on Ariel. She was born on June tenth, 2013. She's four fucking years old, Marie. But she's so tiny."

His voice was strained and shook me to my core. Four years old? Then I realized that he'd dropped an f bomb and frowned up at him. "Scout, you're going to have to quit swearing around her. When she does start talking, I don't want it to be filled with four-letter words. And that's not good. It can't be healthy she's so small for her age. Have you seen the doctor yet? Asked what we can do?"

"I'm trying, but I'm not used to having to monitor my word choice, babe. Could take me a while. And no, I came straight here. Missed my girl." His gaze flicked from me to Ariel. "Or rather, my girls."

He shrugged a backpack off his shoulder and rested it on the end of the bed before he unzipped the top.

"Ariel? I brought your other toys, too. Would you like them?"

That had her full attention. She sat up, and I followed suit, slipping off the bed to sit in the chair beside it as Ariel gave Scout an enthusiastic nod.

"You know, kiddo, you can talk all you want now? No one's going to get angry or cross at you for making noise."

She dropped her chin and frowned a moment before she flicked her gaze to me.

"That's right, honey. You're truly safe and free to do what you want. Within reason, of course, we want you to be safe. But that's all we want, for you to be safe, healthy and happy. Whatever you want to have or do, just ask us and we'll do what we can to get it for you."

As I'd spoken, Scout had taken out a couple of small rustic wooden dolls that looked like they'd been hand carved. The hair on one was white blonde, like Ariel's, and a deeper blonde on the others, like Sarah's. The clothes were clearly hand sewn. Tears filled my eyes as I realized that Sarah must have made these for Ariel.

"Ariel, did your momma make these for you?"

A tear tracked down her cheek as she nodded and carefully stroked the doll with the darker blonde hair.

"She was very clever, and loved you so much, sweetheart."

She nodded her little head again before she shut the world out, rearranged herself on the mattress so she had the dolls and her rabbit in her lap and started to play a silent game with them. My heart broke even more for her.

"Right, okay then. I'm going to head off and find the doctor. A couple of the brothers are out in the hall keeping watch, so you don't have to worry about a thing. Is there anything you want me to bring you?"

I hadn't eaten since breakfast, and it was already past lunch time.

"I'd love a coffee, and maybe a sandwich or something to eat?"

He leaned over and gave me a kiss. He kept it sweet, but I could sense the tension in him, that he wanted to do so much more. I knew, because I felt the same way.

"I'll see what I can do. Be back as soon as I can."

And then he was gone, and since Donna and Rose had left while I'd been sleeping, it was just me and Ariel. As much as I wanted to talk to her, I held off. She wasn't comfortable enough with me yet to talk to me, so she wouldn't answer anything I asked. It would only make her more uncomfortable. So, I sat back and watched as she played, using nothing more than her imagination with her rabbit and dolls, as I thought about everything that was going to need to change in order for her to fit into my world.

The first thing that popped into my mind was where we would live. When I'd left Scout's house, I'd moved into a small place of my own. It had only been me and I didn't want a huge space that would be empty and take me forever to clean. It was a two bedroom, but the second room was tiny, and full of stuff. It wouldn't be big enough for Ariel and all the things she'd need. And I had no backyard for her to run around in. I remembered Zara telling me all about how she and Mac had bought a house next to Eagle and Silk, and Taz and Flick. How the men had taken down the fences between them so they now had a huge shared yard that, in years to come, meant their kids would have open access to all three homes. That was the kind of thing I had always dreamed of having. Close friends, raising kids together... I focused back on Ariel, so happy playing all by herself in complete silence. How long was it going to take to help this sweet little girl open up to the world? So many things, even simple things, were going to overwhelm her.

Scout

After giving the doc the information about Ariel, he told me he needed to go over his notes on her case then he'd meet with us and discuss what Ariel would need going forward, so I left the hospital and headed toward Marie's Cafe. I was sure the girls were doing fine, but I'd told Marie this morning I'd check in on them, and it was the best place in town to get coffee. *Nothing but the best for my old lady.*

About three seconds after pushing the door open, I had Zara in my face asking about a hundred questions.

"Whoa, girl. Take a breath."

With a shake of her head she stopped, and with her eyes closed, took a deep breath. I watched her closely in case she went down and I needed to catch her. Zara had cataplexy and intense emotion could make her drop like a stone as her muscles gave out.

"How is Marie? And the little girl?"

I wasn't sure how much information had filtered down the grapevine so I took her elbow and guided her over to a seat. There were only a few customers in the place and Mercedes looked to have them under control.

"Sarah passed away this morning. The little girl was her daughter, her name's Ariel. We've just found out she's four years old, but she looks about two. Sweet little thing, white blonde hair and big, hazel eyes. I've got things rolling for Marie and me to adopt her."

Tears glistened in her eyes. "Oh, that poor baby. How's Marie holding up?"

"As well as can be expected. I think having Ariel to look after is actually helping her."

A thoughtful expression passed over her face that made me a little nervous. Zara plotting usually meant trouble.

"What are you plotting in that pretty little head of yours now?"

She blinked her eyes for a moment. "No plotting, well, no *bad* plotting. You know there's a couple places for sale on our street right now? If you moved in there, we'd all be close by and the kids could grow up together. We can do play dates."

I gave her a nod as I ran my hand through my hair. "Not a bad idea, Zara. Not sure how long it'll be before Ariel's going to be ready for play dates, though. I don't think she's even met another child before. She doesn't speak. We heard her whispering to Sarah this morning, but other than that, she hasn't said a word."

She started blinking really fast. "Oh, that poor little love."

"Pretty much. Anyhow, I can't stay long, but Marie's hungry and wants coffee. Can you fix her up something?"

She just about leapt from the chair. "I can totally do that."

I sat back as she rushed over and got to work behind the counter. As I waited, I pulled out my phone and Googled up the real estate listings for Bridgewater to find the places Zara mentioned. I knew when Eagle, Mac and Taz all bought next to each other on the one street they'd hoped other brothers would follow their lead and eventually the club would own the whole street. The more I thought about it, the more I liked the idea. Both houses looked good online. Later I'd go visit the agent and see if I could go have a look at them. I wondered if I should take Marie with me or make it a surprise.

Reaching for my bandana, I winced and moved to stroke my beard instead. As much as I liked the idea of surprising her, with Ariel to consider, maybe it would be best if Marie was more involved. And with all the cooking she did, she'd want to check out the kitchen of anywhere we lived. With my mind made up, I decided to visit the agent on my way to the hospital to pick up the printed material they had on the two properties.

Zara came over with a large take-out box and two coffee cups.

"Here you go, just how she likes it. And there's enough for her to share with you, and here's a coffee."

I reached for my wallet and Zara scoffed at me. "Don't you dare try to pay. This is Marie's Cafe, her old man shouldn't have to pay for a coffee any more than Marie should. Go take care of her and let her know we've got everything here covered."

I leaned down to press a kiss to her temple. "You're a treasure, darlin', and I'm glad Mac snapped you up so we get to keep you in the family."

As she blushed a bright red, I left the cafe with my cargo and loaded up my cage. After a quick stop at the real estate agent, I made my way back to the hospital.

When I got to Ariel's room, the little girl was still busy playing with her toys, lost in a world no one but she could see. It was the most normal thing I'd seen her do. Well, normal except for the fact she was doing it in complete silence.

"Hey, babe. The girls made us a meal to share apparently. No f—" I coughed to cover the fact I nearly dropped another f bomb. "I've got no idea what they made, though. Oh, and a coffee."

I handed over the cup and she took a long drink before closing her eyes on a moan. A sound that had my cock hard and ready for her.

"Darlin' you gotta stop that."

She flicked her gaze to mine and a blush stained her cheeks. Yeah, she knew what she'd just done to me. Cheeky woman. I took a mouthful of my own brew.

"Listen, I gotta head back for church. Not sure how long that'll take but I'll come back to get you after, so we can head home. Donna will be back to spend the night with Ariel."

She stood from her seat and wrapped her arms around my waist, snuggling into me. I wound my arms around her and pressed a kiss to the top of her head.

"I've got something to show you tonight, too. Something Zara suggested we might want."

She looked up at me expectantly, but I wasn't gonna tell her yet. Wondering what I was talking about would give her something else to think about during the afternoon. I leaned down and took her mouth. The kiss turned hot fast and it took all my control to end it and not drag her off somewhere so I could take her.

"I can't wait for tonight."

"Me, too."

With a groan, I forced myself to rise from the seat and leave the room. Church was gonna be the shortest on record if I had anything to do with it.

Chapter 11

Marie

When Scout returned, he came back with Donna, who was going to stay with Ariel for the night. As soon as she entered the room, I rose to give her a hug.

"Thank you so much for doing this."

"No need to thank me, honey. We're family, and I think it'll be good to get Ariel used to a few people early on. You can't be awake and by her side twenty-four/seven going forward."

That left me fighting a wince. I did want to be able to care for Ariel by myself, but Donna was right. I was going to need help if I wanted to have any kind of relationship with Scout, and if I wanted to keep my business running.

While lost in my head, Scout managed to get me out of the building and into his car. I watched his face as he began to drive out of the parking lot. He really was a handsome man. The gray in his hair and beard only added to his appeal, at least to me. I was tempted to reach over and run my fingers through his beard or hair, but I didn't want to distract him from driving.

"I figured we could drop by your place so you can pack up some stuff to bring back to mine, then when we get to mine, I'll show you what I told you about earlier."

I chewed my lip for a moment before I spoke. "Is this you asking me to move in with you?"

He shrugged and glanced over at me briefly.

"Your place isn't big enough for all three of us, mine is. Just figured it was logical that you come live with me, then when Ariel gets released from hospital, she can move right in to her own room. Knowing it had been her momma's room once might help her, too."

That was a sweet thought and I agreed that Ariel would like sleeping where her mother had once. But his kitchen was going to need a huge upgrade for me to cook all that I needed to for the cafe. Before I could tell him that, we pulled up to my place. It was small, but it was mine, and it had a state of the art kitchen. I could have bought a larger place, I certainly had the money saved up. But I loved having something smaller that was easier to maintain, and didn't make me feel so lonely by having a ton of empty space everywhere.

I was extremely grateful to see my car was parked in the driveway.

"Do you have my keys?"

"Ah, shit. Yeah. I keep forgetting to give you your stuff back. I swear it's not on purpose."

That had me chuckling as he dug into his pocket while he got out of his car. By the time he joined me on my side of the car, he had them ready and pressed them into my palm.

"I know you don't do it on purpose. We've both got a lot going on right now. You know, if you want, you can head home and I'll pack up my car and come over in a bit."

"No way in hell, Marie. I ain't leaving you alone."

"You will let me bring my car over, though? I need to be able to get myself around when you're busy with club business."

He winced and I suspected he was grinding his teeth for a few moments before he answered.

"Yeah, okay."

I moved to press myself against his front, going up on tip toes to press a kiss to his mouth.

"Thank you, Charlie."

I loved how he melted when I used his birth name. I realized it was playing a little dirty right now but I knew he didn't like the idea of me having my car at his place. He'd no doubt rather drive me everywhere I needed to go, but I'd been living alone and doing everything for myself for a very long time. I didn't want to change that part of myself. As much as I loved Scout, and wanted a relationship with him, I would never become a kept woman who would need him every moment of the day. And I honestly didn't think that was the type of woman Scout needed, either.

"I know I'm being over-protective, babe, but after the last couple of days, I can't help it. I swear, I won't normally be hovering around you all the damn time. I know you enjoy your independence, and I don't want to take that from you. Just give me a week or two to get over nearly losing you, okay?"

My heart melted a little more for him. How could I stay mad at him when he said things like that?

"Deal. C'mon. I want to get this done and see what this surprise is that you've been teasing me with all afternoon."

He followed me once I unlocked the front door and growled when I tossed my keys on the side table.

"What's wrong?"

"Where's your security system, babe?"

I pointed to the lock on the door. "There."

He closed his eyes and tilted his head up for a minute, then with a shake of his head, he looked me in the eye.

"It's a miracle you haven't had any trouble, Marie. You should have some kind of system to monitor the house."

"Scout, I can't sneeze without one of your boys knowing about it. I didn't think wasting money on a fancy system was necessary when I have an entire MC watching my every move."

His expression softened a little as he came to me and pulled me in close before he wrapped his arms around me.

"You've never had someone watching your every move, babe. I know it seemed like it, but I fucking swear, I never put a twenty-four/seven guard on you."

Before I could say anything else, he took my mouth with his in a passionate kiss that left me gripping his sides while my toes curled into the soles of my shoes. His palms slid down to cup my ass and when he lifted me, I wrapped my legs around his waist while he kept kissing me as he pushed me up against the wall. As I wrapped my arms around him and buried my hands in his hair, he shifted one hand from my ass up under my shirt, pulling the cup of my bra down so he could tease my nipple with tweaks and light pinches.

With a groan, I threw my head back against the wall, and Scout moved to kiss his way down my throat, his beard tickling as he moved.

"Missed you today."

"We only spent a few hours apart."

He pulled back and lowered my feet to the ground a moment before he was tearing my shirt off over my head and attacking the fly of my pants.

"I haven't been inside you for-fucking-ever, babe. Need to take you before I lose my fucking mind."

I couldn't form words to respond. The heat and desperation in his eyes and movements were enough to tell me he really was on edge and needed me to bring him back down. I toed off my shoes and shoved my jeans the rest of the way down as he ripped into his own pants. The moment he freed his thick erection, he was back on me, lifting me up against the wall and impaling me on his hard length. I was still a little tender from the previous night, so I felt every ridge of his dick as he slid in deep.

"Oh, Charlie..."

He began to pump in and out of me as he recaptured my mouth. When he moved a palm from my hip back to my breast, I lowered my leg so I could use my foot against the floor to keep up with his thrusts. I wanted him deeper, needed more of him. With a growl he pulled out of me. I whimpered at the sudden loss of his heat, but he spun me around and suddenly I was lying face down over my kitchen table.

"Spread those legs for me, baby."

I did as he asked and a second later, he slammed back home, deeper than before. The head of his dick rubbed against a spot that lit up my insides like the Fourth of July.

"Scout! Charlie!"

"Oh, yeah. Got you now, babe."

He changed his thrusts so every stroke rubbed over that super sensitive spot. My arousal skyrocketed so fast my head spun. I slapped my sweaty palms against the timber of the table as he held fast to my hips and continued to drive me mad with his every stroke. Before I was ready for it, my orgasm rolled through me, sweeping me up and blanking my mind.

Scout

The moment her pussy clenched down on my cock and she cried out my name, a tingle shot down my spine and straight into my balls. Then I was coming, filling my woman up with my seed. As I did, all the stress from my day disappeared.

Taking a deep breath, I lowered my head to kiss my way up her spine as she lay limp across the table. When all she did was moan, I couldn't help but chuckle a little. She was so fucking adorable.

Pulling free from her heat, I tucked myself away and did up my pants, then I lifted her in my arms and made my way toward the back of her house where I knew her bedroom was. I laid her on her bed and ducked into her bathroom to wet a cloth to clean her up.

When I moved her legs so I could wipe her flesh, she moaned and wriggled against the mattress. She must have had one hell of an orgasm to still be so wiped out from it. I made fast work of cleaning her, before I tossed the cloth back into the bathroom and laid down beside her, running my hands over her sexy as fuck body.

When her eyes fluttered open, I leaned in to kiss her gently. Just when I was about to speak, her doorbell rang.

"Ah, fuck. I'll go see who that is while you get dressed. I want you in my bed where I can take my time with you."

Her lips stretched into a lazy smile. "You just had me."

"Yeah, and it wasn't enough. It's never going to be enough, babe."

I gave her another fast kiss before I forced myself to leave her alone.

"If this isn't something fucking important, I'm gonna kill whoever is on the other side of that door."

I'd mumbled the words, but when I heard Marie's chuckle, I figured she'd heard me. With a shake of my head I pulled the door open and caught a glimpse of a man running down the street. He looked vaguely familiar and I stepped forward to go after him when I stubbed my toe on a heavy box sitting on the doorstep. There was nothing written on it, no address or name. It sure as fuck wasn't some FedEx delivery. I glanced up to the fleeing man in time to see him face me and lift his arm to point something at me.

"Ah, fuck."

Reality came crashing down on me and in a flash I was back in the house and shoving the door closed as I attempted to get further down the hall. I only made it two steps before a loud boom filled the air. Then before I could do a fucking thing about it, the force of the explosion had the door splintering a moment before I was thrown down the hallway, crashing hard against the wall.

Eerie silence filled the air while stabs of pain lit up all over my body. When my vision began to dim, I tried to focus down the hallway, to see if Marie was safe, but I only caught a glimpse of her before everything went dark.

Marie

My ears were already ringing when the floor boards under my feet shook as the second explosion blew. I'd been nearly dressed when the first explosion shook my house about a minute ago. Slamming my feet into my shoes, I ran for the hallway, praying Scout was okay.

"Holy shit!"

My hallway looked like a war zone. My front door had been blasted open, splinters of wood from the lower part of the door that was now missing a large chunk, were lodged in the walls and all over the floor, along with nails and bits of metal. My gaze caught on Scout and a gasp slipped from my throat. He was laying out cold on his front, his hand stretched out like he was trying to get to me. I prayed he was only unconscious.

Pulling my phone from my pocket, I rushed to Scout as I dialed Bulldog. Scout had made me promise to call the club first if anything happened, and I didn't intend to break that vow. Of course, the second I finished with him I'd be calling 911.

I put my fingers against his throat, sighing in relief at the strong pulse I found.

"Hey, Marie, what's up?"

I struggled to hear him over the line. "The front of my house just blew up. Scout's out cold."

"Fuck. Hang on." I could just make out his words as he told someone to call 911 and get them out to my house before he returned to speak to me. "Marie? Are you safe? Is anyone else there? Who set the bomb?"

Tears were pricking my eyes but I sucked them down. This wasn't the time. I could break down later.

"My doorbell rang and Scout went to answer it. I wasn't with him. I don't know what happened. There were two explosions. I don't have a front door anymore and Scout has…" I looked closer at Scout's back and legs. "Oh, fuck. He has nails in him, Bulldog! How the hell did he get nails in him?"

Bulldog let lose a string of curses before he calmed enough to talk to me.

"Someone packed a bomb with nails. When it exploded it would have shot out the nails in all directions. Have you been hurt at all?"

I shook my head before remembering he couldn't see me. "No, I was in another room."

"Okay, do you have a weapon? A gun?"

"I don't know what to do with a gun." That suddenly seemed like a massive oversight. I glanced around, looking for something, anything I could use as a weapon. I stood and ran to the kitchen and pulled out the largest blade from my knife block. "Okay, I have a knife. It's all I have."

"That's fine, darlin'. If anyone you don't know comes at you, stab first, ask questions later, okay?"

"All right."

I had no idea if I could stab someone and I hoped like hell I wouldn't have to find out. The sound of boots crunching just outside had me gripping the knife tighter as I whispered into the phone.

"Someone's here. Just outside."

"Arrow and Nitro are on their way, Marie. They should be there any second, can you see anything?"

I stood and crept a little closer to the front door and gasped at what I saw. But before I could process the state of Scout's car, Nitro and Arrow both came into view.

"It's them. I'm safe. Thank you Bulldog."

"Okay, darlin', I'm gonna hang up and get moving over there myself. Stick with Nitro and Arrow and I'll see you soon."

Hanging up the phone, I put the knife down on the side table next to my keys as I took a few deep breaths, relieved when I could hear the sound of approaching sirens.

"Marie? You doing okay?"

I turned to Arrow and before I knew what I was doing, I was sobbing against his hard chest. I'd known Arrow for over ten years, knew he was safe, knew he'd keep Scout and me protected. His large hands rubbed my back as he made soothing noises for a few minutes. I couldn't hear him, but could feel the vibrations through his chest. He kept hold of me as he turned toward where Scout was.

"Brother? How is he?"

"He's breathing, strong pulse. But he's got fucking shrapnel embedded everywhere."

With a final sniffle, I pulled away from Arrow to go to Scout. Kneeling beside him on the floor, I stroked his hair off his face, praying he'd wake up. When I ran my knuckles over his cheek, he frowned and groaned. Relief poured through me and I leaned down to press a kiss to his cheek.

"Stay still, Scout. You'll hurt yourself if you move."

I didn't want him to try to stand and injure himself even more by moving all the metal and wood that was currently embedded into his body.

He tensed and his eyes flicked open and I could see the panic in his eyes. Arrow knelt down next to me and lifted his hand in a stop gesture, then clenched his hand into a fist, gave Scout a nod and a thumbs up sign.

"He won't be able to hear you, Marie, no matter how loud you yell."

I frowned up at him. "I'm yelling?"

He smirked at me. "Yeah, darlin'. Don't worry, it's normal when you can't hear well to yell. If you aim to speak at what sounds like a whisper to yourself, you should be about right in volume."

My cheeks heated with embarrassment as I realized I must have been yelling at Bulldog on the phone earlier. Poor man, his ears were probably ringing worse than mine!

Suddenly my house filled with people in uniforms and I watched in shock as they got Scout onto a gurney and out the door. A medic came and spoke to me but I was focused on Scout, not caring about myself. I vaguely heard Arrow tell them he'd make sure I got to the hospital soon. I tried to follow the medics that had Scout but before I could, a police officer got in my face and started asking questions. Arrow stopped him speaking before I could answer him.

"No way is she answering you right now. She needs to go to the hospital to get her ears checked. The blast has left her with impaired hearing."

A look of sympathy crossed the man's face before he moved aside and let me pass. I followed Arrow outside and stopped frozen in place as I got a good look at Scout's car. What the hell had happened to it? The hood was sitting beside the car and the front wheels were at an odd angle.

"At a guess, the second explosion was a bomb set under the hood. Don't think we're gonna be able to fix it. Scout's gonna be pissed that both his bike and car have been damaged within days of each other."

Not wanting to yell anymore, I simply nodded and let him lead me away from the wreck.

Chapter 12

Marie

After a full week of living at the Charon MC clubhouse, I was over it. I understood that it was for my own safety, especially with Scout still in hospital. But it was still frustrating to be so confined. Everyone was on edge, waiting for the bomber to do something else, but he hadn't so far.

I was also beyond tired because I couldn't sleep in Scout's bed on my own. I couldn't help but wonder how many of the club whore's he'd had in here. Plus, the sheets smelled of him, and everything in his room reminded me of him, but *he* wasn't here. I couldn't reach for him. Touch him, have him touch me. At least it was nearly over. Today Scout was set to get released from hospital. I'd thankfully not needed to stay myself, as my hearing cleared up within a few hours of the blasts. Scout had gotten lucky with his hearing too. By the morning after the blasts, his hearing had return to the point he could hear, but it sounded like he was under water. By the third day, it was back to normal. I was so grateful we'd both escaped having any permanent damage to our ears.

However, since the bomb had been filled with nails and had blown out part of my wooden door, Scout had ended up with nails and large splinters embedded up the back of his body. He'd put his hands over his head, so thankfully didn't have any damage to his skull. But it was because of those pieces of shrapnel that he'd had to stay face down on a hospital bed until the doctor was happy with how the wounds were healing.

This hadn't suited my man one bit. Nope, Scout did not make a good patient. Like most men, he was grumpy as hell and hated that he couldn't go hunt down the bastard who had tried to blow us up. I was extremely glad he was in hospital and not home, where I'd have to try to keep him contained. The nurses needed some kind of medal for not tying him to the bed and gagging him.

Little Ariel was ready to come home too. Well, she'd been ready to be released for a few days now but the club had struck a deal with the doctor that meant Ariel could stay until Scout was ready to come home. We'd all agreed having her living in the clubhouse wasn't a good idea. It was too similar to where she'd been living with lots of men around all the time and tiny rooms.

Despite the fact that whenever I left the building I had biker shadows, I still managed to make a few trips out to shop for Ariel and to go over to Scout's house to get her room set up. Rose and Donna had been a huge help, and we put our guards to good use when it came to heavy lifting.

When I got to the hospital, I went to Scout's room first. If something had happened and he wasn't being released today after all, I didn't want Ariel to have to be shuffled around unnecessarily. I also wanted Scout with me when we went to get Ariel to bring her home. I wanted to start how I planned to continue. Scout and me, together with Ariel.

I stopped short when I entered Scout's room, taking in the sight before me. Scout was standing near the bed, dressed only in jeans with his back towards the door. I tried to look past the fresh red scars that were now dotted over his back, but it was hard to ignore them and the way they stood out against his large tattoo of the Charon insignia. I guessed he'd be going to see Silk once the scars fully healed so she could touch up his ink. Once I managed to pull my gaze from his new scars, I could tell his whole body was tense, and with the way he had his hands on his hips I could tell he was glaring at the poor nurse who was standing in front of him and trying to tell him something.

"Scout, are you giving this poor woman a hard time for doing her job?"

His body stayed still for a moment before he spun and lunged toward me. Gathering me up tight against him, he pressed a kiss to the top of my head as he stroked his palms up and down my back and sides. Peace filled me instantly. I'd missed being in his arms so much. It seemed crazy that I'd become so addicted to him in such a short time, but it was the truth. I needed his touch and presence in my world for it to be right. For the past week all I'd been able to do is stroke his face or hold his hand. With a small sigh, I rested my palms on his hips, careful not to reach behind him, where I risked hurting one of his wounds.

"Where's your escort, love? You know you can't just go wandering around on your own right now."

I rolled my eyes and twisted my way out of his grip. "Keg's out in the waiting room. Well, technically he's at the reception desk flirting his heart out with the new admin." I turned to the nurse. "So, what does he need to do to keep healthy?"

The poor woman seemed relieved to be able to tell me what Scout needed to do. Scout had really given the woman hell. I quietly listened to all her instructions, then took the scripts from her for antibiotics he still needed to take, and some pain pills which I was sure he'd refuse to take. Then she had him sign his discharge papers and he was free to go. As soon as he'd returned her pen, the poor woman just about ran from the room. After she left, I frowned over at Scout.

"You didn't have to scare the poor woman so much. She's just doing her job."

He looked a little sheepish for a moment before he gave me a wide grin. "Don't be mad, babe. I've never been a good patient. I hate being stuck inside at the best of times. Being stuck lying on my damn front for a fucking week when I wanted to be out there hunting this fucker made it even worse."

I ignored his comment about hunting for now and gave him another eye roll. "Yeah, I caught that. C'mon, hurry up and get dressed already. We need to go get Ariel."

"Then we get to go home."

His look was hot enough my nipples went hard and warmth grew in my lower belly, but I did my best to push the arousal down.

"I wouldn't get too excited. We're going to have a young child in the house, so there'll be no throwing me up against the wall until after her bed time from now on."

He growled as he tugged a shirt from the bag I'd brought him yesterday and pulled it over his head. He eased his cut on over his broad shoulders then zipped up the bag. I went to take it off the bed when he grabbed me and tossed me on the bed. Before I could say a word, he was on top of me, his thick thigh pushed between my legs and pressed against my core as he took my mouth with his. He licked at my lips until I opened for him, then he deepened the kiss. My arousal skyrocketed under his assault. Eventually I had to twist my head to the side, breaking the fiery kiss in order to catch a breath. He nibbled at my ear before he spoke.

"We'll find a way, babe. It's been a long fucking week since I've been inside you, Marie. I ain't waiting till nightfall to take what's mine."

He had me so heated up I was thinking pulling our pants down right here on the hospital bed was a good idea. Until a knock on the door interrupted things and brought reality back into focus.

"Who is it?"

I figured it wouldn't be a nurse or doctor as they didn't knock, but I didn't want to be caught by one of his brothers like this either. I wriggled and managed to get myself out from under him just as Keg called out.

"You both all right in there?"

"Yeah, we'll be out in a sec."

Scout then mumbled something about cock blocking brothers but I pretended like I didn't hear him as I dashed into the bathroom to finger comb my hair and attempt to get my body under control. Damn man turned my mind to mush with his kisses.

When I came out a minute or two later, Scout was in the hallway chatting with Keg. Taking a deep breath, I held my head high and went over to them.

"Right, let's go get Ariel so we can get out of here. I'm so over hospitals."

Scout chuckled. "You and me both, babe."

I was grateful all the paperwork had been handled and somehow Scout had called in favors to get the courts to fast-track our adoption of Ariel. Well, we were technically her foster parents for the moment, but Arrow had assured me that it wouldn't be long before we got the final word on us adopting her.

It didn't take us long to make our way over to Ariel's room. She sat on the bed, silently playing with her rabbit and dolls again. It was completely adorable, and totally heartbreaking to watch her play. She looked so much like Sarah that every time I looked at her my heart ached for my lost sister. Watching her play, it reminded me that I still needed to finalize the funeral for Sarah. It was another thing that had been put off until after Scout and Ariel were out of hospital and back home. I bit back a groan as my mental to-do list got longer and longer by the second.

"You okay, babe?"

Scout wrapped an arm around me and I cuddled up against his side. "Yeah, just thinking about everything I need to do."

With a finger under my chin, he tilted my face up so he could give me a short, sweet kiss.

"You're not alone, Marie. I'll be standing by your side for every one of those things on your list. As will the club."

That made me smile. This man was as perfect as I'd always imagined he would be, and I was so damn happy he was finally mine.

Scout

Even with the few things the old ladies had brought in for Ariel over the time she'd been here, the kid didn't have much. Ariel's face lit up when Marie showed her the bright pink backpack she'd bought her. With a grin, I stood back and watched as Marie helped Ariel pack. The little girl carefully placed each of her possessions inside the bag as though each one were made of fine crystal. Bulldog had told me during the week how the old ladies had gone out with Marie a few times to buy a ton of shit for the kid, then taken it all back to my place. As much as I was dreading seeing how much pink they'd filled my house up with, I couldn't wait to see what she was going to do with all her new things. Although, I still thought I should have a little chat with the old ladies about spoiling the girl. She needed to be eased into the real world, not thrown in the deep end where she'd suffocate from all the attention and stuff suddenly surrounding her. However, when I'd mentioned that to Bulldog earlier he'd just rolled his eyes at me and told me the women all knew that already and there was nothing I could say that would change the fact that Ariel was gonna be spoiled with both attention and gifts.

"Right, we're all packed and ready to go, Ariel. Are you ready to come see your new home?"

The little girl clutched her bag and looked both worried and nervous. I went over and kneeled down in front of her, so she could look into my eyes.

"Hey, Ariel, you know where we're going, right? To my house? You remember Marie telling you how the three of us are all going to be living in the same house? Just you, Marie and me. No one else. You're even gonna have your own room and Marie's bought you a few things so you'll be comfortable. Does that sound good?"

She still looked worried and I wasn't sure what she needed to feel better. What would have her so worried still? Then it hit me. She'd lived in fear of one man her whole life.

"You remember us saying how you'll be safe with us? It was the truth. Bruce is gone forever. You won't ever have to see any of the men from where you used to live again. My house is very safe. It has a special security system with an alarm that will make a really loud noise if anyone comes in who shouldn't."

The more I spoke the more relaxed she looked, until finally she glanced to Marie and gave her a small nod. My woman knew what the little girl needed, she came straight over and took her hand. Then we were walking out of the room and toward the entrance of the hospital, Keg walking in front of us to make sure nothing nasty was waiting for us outside.

When we got to Marie's car, Ariel stopped short of the vehicle.

"You ever been in a car before, darlin'?"

She shook her head at my question and I cursed silently. Of course she hadn't.

"Well, how about Scout sits in the back with you while I drive us?" Before I could protest against her driving, she held her palm up at me. "No way are you driving after all the medications you've been on for the past week, so don't even try it."

Knowing she was right didn't mean I had to like it. She continued to talk to Ariel about how the car worked and how long we'd be inside it while she got her buckled into the new booster seat. Leaving her to it, I went to speak with Keg.

"What's the plan?"

"You know we had Marie living in your room at the clubhouse while you were in here but nothing's happened all week. That don't mean it won't though, so I'll follow you back to your place and hang out to keep guard until nightfall, when someone else will come take over. Not sure who Nitro lined up. No matter what, you and Marie will have at least one of us outside whatever building you're in until we find this fucker."

I gave him a nod then when I noticed that Marie was ready to go, I walked back to the car and leaned down to speak with Ariel.

"So, kiddo, is it all right if I sit back here with you?"

She gave me a little nod as she kept a tight grip on her new bag. Without another word, I climbed in and sat next to the little girl who was, for all intents and purposes, my daughter. I stopped breathing for a moment as the realization hit me. Adopting Ariel meant she was mine. My daughter. I was a fucking dad. Holy shit. I glanced over at her just as Marie started the car and she jumped and tensed in her seat. Automatically I reached my hand over to rest on her little knee.

"It's okay, Ariel. Cars make that noise when they're turned on."

For the entire trip home I explained about how motors worked and why they made the noises they did. By the time we pulled up in my driveway, her little hand was wrapped around one of my fingers and she was intently watching me as I spoke.

Kid was a sponge and clearly wanted to know more. I could easily see her with me at the shop, helping strip down a bike motor. With a grin, I pulled my hand free and undid her seat belt as Marie opened her door.

"Here we are, little darlin'. Home sweet home."

Keeping an eye on my girls, I climbed out and moved to follow them up the path to the front door. I patted my pockets and bit back the growl when I didn't find anything. I still had no fucking phone, hadn't had time to get a new one, and Marie had my keys. Glancing around the yard and house, I waited as Marie unlocked the door and led Ariel inside. As Marie punched in the code, I spoke up.

"Stay here for a minute. I want to do a quick check."

Marie rolled her eyes but didn't say anything as I took off to do a sweep of the house to make sure no one had been inside. I couldn't help but wince when I got to Ariel's room. I'd been right and it was like a pink and purple bomb had gone off, covering everything with color. As much as I was sure Ariel would love it, I was glad I wouldn't have to sleep in there. It was enough to give a man nightmares.

Finding nothing out of place, I made my way back to my girls.

"All clear. Ready to see your room?"

Ariel gave me a nod as she clung to Marie's hand. I couldn't wait for her to be comfortable enough with us to talk. There was something unnatural about a small child being so damn quiet.

I trailed behind them as Marie took her down the hallway toward her new bedroom. As we went, Marie explained how the room had been her mother's years ago. Her little head did another nod, then when we got the room, she stopped short and I moved so I could see her face. I smirked at her wide eyes and open mouth.

"Go on in, Ariel. This is your space, you can do whatever you like in here. If you don't like anything we've put in here, just tell us and we'll fix it up."

She slowly stepped into the room, running her fingers over the books on the bookshelf before she went over to the bed that was made up with a pretty unicorn blanket and at least half a dozen various shaped pillows. Marie moved over to my side and I wrapped an arm around her shoulder to pull her in against me. My heart swelled as we stood there watching Ariel pull out her rabbit and dolls from her bag to sit on the bed. Standing here, watching my daughter settle into her room, it occurred to me that in this moment all was right in my world, now that I had both my girls here in my home with me.

Now if we could just catch this fucker who had tried to blow us up, I'd be a completely happy man.

Chapter 13

Scout

The next morning I woke up feeling better than I had in a week. I'd rapidly gotten used to sleeping with Marie in my arms and it had fucking sucked to not have her with me while I was stuck in that fucking hospital bed. Not that we did a whole lot of sleeping when I did finally get her back in my bed.

Ariel had worn herself out with all the excitement by mid-afternoon and had laid down in her bed and fallen asleep. So I'd tossed Marie over my shoulder and carried her off to our room to make good on my earlier promise. Then after we'd eaten dinner, we'd all sat together on the sectional sofa and Marie read Ariel a story before I had to carry the sleepy little girl up to her room. Clearly, sitting in the back of the car with her had won me some serious points because no way would she have let me pick her up and carry her like that before now, yet she happily clung to me as I took her to bed, then tucked her in under all the blankets. I'd pressed a kiss to her temple and wished her good night. She still hadn't spoken, but I had gotten a little smile out of her. Marie had then given her a similar kiss and followed it up by reminding her where our room was and that if she got scared she could come find us at any time. She also reminded Ariel of the night light in the hall and bathroom so she could find her way in the dark.

That reminded me, I needed to buy stuff to set up an alarm of some kind so we'd know if she was about to come interrupt us. Last thing I wanted was to scar the poor kid by having her walk in on me working over Marie one night.

Marie, with Ariel trailing behind her, walking into the kitchen caught my attention and brought me out of my thoughts. Damn, my woman was beautiful. She'd looked so worn out yesterday but today she looked a lot more refreshed and happier, like maybe she hadn't been able to sleep without me by her side either. *Comforting thought that I wasn't the only one in this relationship that was so fucking far gone.*

She looked around the room with a wince.

"What's up, babe?"

"If I'm moving in here, we'll need to update this kitchen. It'll take me forever to do all the cafe baking with these old appliances."

"Yeah, about that. I never did get to tell you about that surprise I had for you, did I?"

She pulled down a bowl and showed Ariel the cereal options that hadn't been there last week.

"No, you didn't. To be honest, with everything that's happened, I'd forgotten all about it. So, what is it?"

I grinned when Ariel pointed to the tiger on the blue Frosted Flakes box. Only a child would pick her cereal based on the fact it had a cute picture on the box. Marie poured it into the bowl, added milk then seated Ariel at the table like she'd been doing this mom thing for years, not days. Fuck, she was such a natural.

She frowned over at me. "What's that goofy grin for?"

"Just sitting here enjoying watching you do this mom thing like a pro, babe."

A blush colored her cheeks as she flustered around putting the milk away and wiping down the already clean bench. I decided to cut her a break and take the focus off her for a bit.

"The surprise was a new house."

Her head snapped over to look at me and her eyes were wide open. I couldn't help but chuckle as Ariel gave me the same look.

"There's a couple places on the market on the same street as Mac, Eagle and Taz. I know this place is old, and I haven't put the time into keeping it maintained over the years. Also, there's safety in us all buying places close together. We're hoping eventually we'll own all the houses on the street. It'll also mean we're closer to the other kids, for when Ariel is ready."

Ariel frowned and returned to eating her cereal as I'd spoken, but Marie was smiling.

"That sounds wonderful. Are you sure you want to leave this place? I know it's your family home. We can easily fix up the things that need it."

That had me grinning again. She was so fucking sweet. "This is just a house, babe. It's having you and Ariel in it that makes it a home. I'll call the agent this morning and see if we can go around and have a look later today."

Ariel was still frowning and I wasn't sure what had her worried. This no talking thing was highly fucking aggravating when it came to working out what the kid was thinking. Before I could figure out something to say there was a knock on the door so I rose to go answer it, leaving Marie with Ariel.

I opened the door to find Keys had come baring gifts.

"Hey, brother, good to see you back on your feet. Got some stuff for you."

"Come on in. The girls are in the kitchen. Want a coffee?"

"Sure. If Marie's moved in, there's a chance it's not the shit you normally stock your kitchen with."

"Bastard." I gave him a light punch in the arm as we made our way back to the kitchen. He was right, Marie had stocked the kitchen with all sorts of goodies I hadn't bothered buying in years.

"Hey, Keys, how are you doing? Want a coffee?"

"I'm good, and coffee sounds like heaven if you're making it."

He went over and gave her a quick hug and a peck on the cheek before he moved to sit next to me at the table.

"Quit flirting with my woman, already. You said you had presents?"

I fucking hoped he had a new phone for me.

He raised an eyebrow at me. "Cranky this morning, aren't you? Thought you'd be in a better mood, considering." His gaze zeroed in on Ariel. "And how are you this morning, sweetheart? Did you like your new room?"

She gave him a quick nod before focusing back on her breakfast. She'd finished her cereal and Marie had put a small bowl of cut up fruit with some yogurt in front of her. The doctor had explained that we needed to keep her eating lots of healthy food so she would hopefully catch up to where she should be, size-wise. The way she ploughed through food had me thinking we weren't ever going to have an issue getting this kid to eat. Keys gave her a sad smile before turning back to me.

"Right, so here's your new phone. Same number. When those f—ah, men wrecked your phone, they didn't damage the SIM so you have all your old contacts and stuff."

I tried not to laugh at Keys trying to not swear as he spoke. It was good to know I wasn't the only one struggling to clean up my language.

"Thanks, brother. You get a look at my bike and cage?"

"Yeah, your bike needs a lot of work but it's fixable. You'll have her back on the road in a week or so at my guess, but your cage is toast. They somehow managed to climb under the front end and plant that bomb up against the engine. Sorry brother, but there's no fixing that shit."

He winced at Marie after he swore. "Sorry, Marie. Trying to not curse."

"I know, Keys. You're doing good."

I ran my hand through my hair. "Well, that's going to be fun to explain to the damn insurance company."

Keys shrugged. "This is a rare occasion where, since the police were involved, we have a police report for the insurance guys. You'll be all right."

Yeah, wasn't that the truth. Normally when one of the club's vehicles got written off, it was because it was involved with something it shouldn't have been. Hard to explain bullet holes and shit like that to an insurance company when you don't have a police report to back shit up.

I looked up at Marie. "What are your plans for today, babe? Mind if I head over to the shop and check out my bike?"

Not that I didn't believe Keys, but I was hoping it wasn't as bad as he'd said it was.

"Donna, Rose and a couple of the other old ladies are going to drop by this morning. We need to finish arranging things for Friday. But aside from that, I figured a quiet day at home was what Ariel and I needed today, so I don't mind at all if you need to go do your thing."

Friday was the funeral. I had no idea how Ariel was going to cope with saying goodbye to her mom. Was four years old too young for her to understand about death? I had no idea, and there wasn't much I could do about it right now.

I turned my attention back to Keys. "You bring a cage or bike?"

"Since I figured you'd want to head over to the shop, I brought a cage." He gave me a smirk. "Although, you riding bitch on the back of my bike would be a sight to see."

I gave him another thump on the shoulder for being an asshole, and froze when Ariel cringed back into her seat.

"Hey, Ariel. It's okay, I didn't hurt Keys, just gave him a little tap for teasing me."

Keys jumped in fast to try to help ease her. "That's right, kiddo. I was teasing Scout and he gave me a tap for it. It didn't hurt because he didn't do it to hurt me. Okay?"

She nodded but didn't exactly look like she believed us. I made a mental note to try to curb the rough-housing with my brothers around her until she got more settled with us. After that, I decided it would best if Keys and I got out of Marie's hair asap.

I rose from the table and went to kneel down beside Ariel.

"I really am sorry I scared you, sweetheart. I promise you I will never hurt you, and I won't ever hurt my friends, either. We just play fight a little here and there."

I leaned in to press a light kiss to the top of her head as I stood, then I moved to Marie and pulled her in for a tight hug and deep kiss. With a groan I pulled back, said goodbye to them both then followed Keys outside. Once we were in the vehicle, Keys spoke up again.

"You doing okay, brother?"

I ran my hand through my hair. "Yeah, it's just—well—fuck. My world has been turned on its fucking head in the past two weeks. I'm just trying to catch up."

He nodded silently for a few moments. "Taking on a child is a big commitment, especially one with issues."

"You did all you could for Emma, brother."

Emma was Donna's daughter who Keys had taken on the role of father with. Then last year, her biological father, a bastard from the Iron Hammers, got to her and convinced her to help him snatch Zara out from under our noses at our clubhouse. He paid her for her help by killing her, leaving her body for us to find.

"I know. Still eats at me, though. I don't think you ever get over losing a child, no matter how old they are or how stupid their decisions were. You love 'em regardless, always holding out hope they'll see the light one day. Once they're gone, there's no hope left."

What the fuck was I going to say to that? I stayed silent, just listening to the noise of the road under the tires until Keys chose to break the silence.

"But it'll be different with Ariel. There's no sperm donor out there waiting to come snatch her out from under your guard and fuck with her head."

"Felt good taking those pieces of shit out. But we didn't take out enough of them, it seems."

"What do you mean?"

"It took me a few days to remember everything that happened before the blast. But now I do. I know who the fucker is who set those charges. It's the youngest of the three we let the cops take in. Donald warned me he was looking like he might come for revenge when he came to tell me he had to let the three of them go."

"Yeah, well, in Donald's defense, it's a little hard to charge someone for something when all the evidence is blown to hell. Not that I'm arguing with how we handled it. That drug needed to be completely destroyed, no fucking doubt about that."

"Don't suppose you can use your skills and get me some information on him?"

"Already done, prez. I had Nitro take photos of every man out there on his phone when they were lined up out the back waiting for you. I did a quick search on all of them, but I did a deeper look into the three we left alive while you were in the hospital. Figured it would be a good idea to keep an eye on them for at least the next year or so."

"So spill. Who is this fucker and where is he?"

"His name is Simon Haus, and at a guess, the reason he's so pissed is because his big brother was one of the men we took out. As to where he's living, I don't have that. The other two stayed at that cheap-ass hotel in town for one night, then they left town. I found them on some security feeds catching a bus from Houston up to Dallas. I don't think either of those boys will cause us any trouble. But Simon has been keeping a nice, low profile.

I can't find any trace of him. Mind you, I didn't realize he was causing shit. Now I do, I'll try some other things to track his ass down. Don't worry, I'll find him."

I scrubbed both my hands over my face before running my hands over my head. The bandana might be gone, but the habit of adjusting it had just morphed to running my hands over my hair now.

"Get Nitro to arrange more brothers to spend more time out and around town. I want our colors all over Bridgewater until we find this bastard."

"I'll give him a call from the shop and get it sorted. You want a smoke? Pretty sure I got a pack of yours in here somewhere."

That had me chuckling. "You know what? I haven't even thought about lighting up since I got rescued."

Pretty sure it was because now, when I wanted to release some stress, I did it by lovin' on my woman, not smoking up some nicotine.

"Good thing, considering Marie would kick your ass if you tried to smoke around her or Ariel."

"Damn straight."

We pulled up to the shop and I slipped out of the car as soon as it stopped. My wounds were all healing well, but they still didn't like having pressure on them, and sitting seemed to put pressure on all the wrong spots. Not that I'd say that out loud. Marie would find out and force the painkillers she'd gotten for me down my throat. Those fuckers knocked me out all night long, which I wasn't having. Nights were for lovin' on my old lady, not sleeping like a passed out drunk.

As soon as I saw my poor bike, all other thoughts left my head.

"Those motherfucking assholes!"

They hadn't just shoved my Harley off the road to hide it. Nope, they'd taken a knife to everything they could. The paintwork was fucked too, but I'd already figured that would be the case. I ran my hand over the leather of the seat, over the rips in the fabric. This was gonna take some serious work to fix. It would take me at least the rest of the day to assess what parts I needed to order, and then it looked like Keys was gonna be proven right in it taking about a week to get it back on the road. It could even take longer, depending on how long it took to get parts in.

Rolling up my sleeves, I got ready to get to work. The sooner I got it started, the sooner I could get it done. And once I had the parts all ordered, I needed to head over to the clubhouse and pick up one of the club's cages, then go and buy another booster seat. Moving the one Marie had between cars was going to get old fast. I had no idea how long the insurance would take to pay up on my cage, but with my bike out of action as well, I needed some way to get around till I got it sorted.

Marie

I'd had a great day so far, relaxing at home with Ariel and a few of the other old ladies. Ariel seemed to be comfortable around Donna and Rose now. When Silk had come over with little Raven, Ariel had been curious enough about the baby to forget about the fact she'd been scared of Silk earlier. It helped that Silk had worn a long sleeve shirt that covered her ink. For some reason her sleeve tattoo freaked the girl out. It seemed strange to me, because she didn't seem to mind the men and their tattoos. By the time we'd sat down to lunch, Ariel had been smiling and pulling faces at Raven, making the six-month-old grin. I thought I'd seen Ariel lean in to whisper a few times, but couldn't be sure.

I'd been grateful when soon after lunch, she slipped down the hall to her room for a nap. It meant we could get the funeral stuff all organized without her overhearing what we were doing. I had no idea how she was going to handle it on Friday, but the least I could do for her was save her from hearing about it all week in the lead up to it.

Now everyone had left, it was just Ariel and me, who'd only woken up from her nap about ten minutes ago. I'd just chopped up an apple for her when Scout came through the front door.

"Hey, honey, I'm home!"

Shaking my head and chuckling, I called back. "We're in the kitchen."

He strolled in and after ruffling Ariel's hair, he came to me and pressed a short, but hot, kiss on my lips.

"Let me go shower and change, then we'll go check out these houses."

Before I could say a thing he was gone again. The man never stopped. With another shake of my head and a chuckle, I turned back to Ariel, who'd now finished eating her snack.

"Would you like to go get a few toys or books to bring with us? We're going to go for another car ride."

She hopped up and headed toward her room with a frown on her face. I had no idea what was wrong. Surely she wasn't upset over going in the car? She'd seemed to enjoy the ride from the hospital with her hand on Scout's as he explained all about how a car worked. Hell, I'd probably learned more from that conversation than Ariel had.

My man didn't waste time in the shower and about ten minutes later, we were all heading out the door.

"You got a new car already?"

"Nah, just grabbed one of the club's cages. It'll take some time for the insurance to come through on mine, and my bike's gonna take me at least a week to get fixed up."

I couldn't hold back the grin when I noticed he'd gone out and bought a second booster seat for Ariel. It would certainly be easier having one in each of our cars so we didn't have to be constantly moving the thing. I quickly strapped Ariel in and she happily started looking over one of the picture books I'd bought her as she clung to her rabbit.

"Ariel? Is it okay if I sit up front with Scout?"

She looked up and gave me a smile and nod before she returned to her book about wild animals. Well, that answered the question about whether it was the car ride that had caused her to be so worried earlier. It also meant I had no damn clue what it had been.

Shaking the thought aside, I moved around the vehicle and climbed into the front passenger seat. As soon as I was buckled in, Scout cranked the engine and took off.

"There's two houses we can look at but I think you'll like this first one better. The second one's kitchen isn't as good."

Warmth filled my heart that he'd listened to me and remembered what I wanted in a house. I reached over and rested my palm on his thigh as he drove.

"I'm sure it'll be great and I can't wait to see it."

It didn't take long to reach the house and the agent was waiting for us when we pulled into the drive. After getting out of the car, I looked up the road to gauge how far we were from the others. Eagle's house was two up on the opposite side of the street.

"You coming inside, babe?"

I turned back to see Scout had picked Ariel up. She looked even smaller than usual in his big arms. I stepped up beside him and ran my palm over Ariel's soft hair. She was looking worried again, clearly something about a new house was bothering her. I really wished she'd just talk to me. It would make it so much easier to help her.

The agent unlocked the door and we followed her in. She was talking non-stop about all the features the house had, but I wasn't really listening. Until I saw the kitchen, I didn't care what was in the rest of the house. Scout obviously picked up on what I needed and asked the agent to skip forward to the kitchen.

"Of course. Please follow me."

She led us through a family room into a spacious, well set up kitchen.

"It truly is a spectacular kitchen. The current owners completely renovated this room about two years ago. I've been told that the husband was training to be a chef and was struggling to practice in the previous kitchen, so he had it gutted and turned into a chef's dream."

"He sure did."

I was nearly giddy with excitement. The stove was huge, with eight burners. It had to be industrial. And a double oven! I pressed my palm over my heart as I ran the other one over the sleek, stainless steel appliance.

The low rumble of Scout's laugh came from behind me. "I think you just sold a house, darlin'. Although, I do believe I might have a struggle on my hands getting her to leave until the paperwork can go through."

The agent chuckled and I had to smile.

"This kitchen is *perfect*. It's even better than the one at my place. So, let's have a look at all the other rooms. Are all the bedrooms upstairs?"

"All but one. There's a guest bedroom with a small, attached bathroom downstairs, then the master and two bedrooms on the upper floor. Shall we head up?"

Part of me didn't want to leave the kitchen until I'd opened every cupboard and appliance to fully check them out, but the rest of me knew we were looking at the whole house, not just the kitchen. My cooking requirements weren't the only consideration. I followed Scout up the stairs and was impressed with how light and airy this top floor was.

"There are two baths up here, one connected to the master bedroom and the other is between the other bedrooms."

Scout bypassed the master bedroom and went down to the others. I wondered what he was up to for a moment, but when I saw Ariel's face and the frown she was sporting, I figured Scout had an idea on how to fix whatever was bothering our little girl.

"So Ariel, you'll get to pick which one you want." He placed her on the ground so she could check out each of the rooms for herself. "It's totally your choice, little darlin', and you can even pick what color we paint the walls for you. It'll be your space, just like your room at my house is now."

By the time she'd thoroughly examined every inch of both rooms and bathroom, she returned to us with a smile on her face. Was that what had been bothering her? She thought she wouldn't have her own room at our new house? Tears pricked my eyes as she took my hand and guided me into the room that faced the backyard, its big window looking out over the trees and grass.

"You want this one, sweetheart?"

She nodded her head and turned to face Scout, checking his reaction.

"Done deal, kiddo. How about we look at the rest of the house, yeah?"

While she was facing away from me, I brushed the tears away and sucked in a breath. This poor little girl had been through so much, but I vowed she'd not suffer like that ever again. She'd always know she was loved and wanted, and I would always make sure she had everything she needed in life.

By the time we left the house twenty minutes later, Scout had put an offer in and the agent had told us she should be able to get back to us if not tonight, then in the morning about whether it was accepted. Scout had also spoken to the woman about putting his place on the market.

As soon as we got home, I took Ariel to her room and popped a movie on the TV there for her to watch. Since she'd never seen a TV before, movies enthralled her thoroughly. Especially this one. The Little Mermaid, her namesake.

With her occupied, that meant I had over an hour to do what I pleased. And what I wanted to do, was Scout. I rushed from the back of the house in search of him and found him grabbing a beer from the fridge in the kitchen.

I took the bottle from his hand and returned it before I took his hand and led him toward the stairs with a grin.

Picking up on what I was after, he growled low in his throat before he scooped me up and ran up the stairs. Once we were inside our bedroom, he put me back on my feet and pressed me against the now closed door.

"Whatcha want, babe?"

"The new place is perfect. I'm so happy, and excited, and overwhelmed… I need to let it all out. I figured what better way to do that than show my man exactly how much I love him."

"How long do we have?"

"Ariel's watching The Little Mermaid, so we have a little over an hour."

His smile was a little wild as he flipped the lock on the door then set about stripping off his clothes.

"Need you naked, babe. If I do it, I'm gonna tear your clothes off."

Before I did as instructed I cupped his bearded jaw between my palms, stilling his movements.

"I love you, Charlie, so much."

Then the man who owned my heart kissed me. As he continued to seduce me with his long, drugging kisses, his hands worked at my clothes. Within minutes I was naked and he was tweaking my nipples as his mouth moved down my neck toward the tight peaks.

"Fucking love you so much, Marie."

He dropped to his knees and nudged my legs apart. I was already on edge, and when he covered my core with his mouth and thrust his talented tongue in deep, I blew apart, banging my head against the door as I came for him.

Before I could come back down, I was on the bed with Scout leaning over me and sliding his thick erection deep inside me. Looked like my man wasn't going to waste one moment of this short time we had to ourselves. And I loved him even more for it.

Chapter 14

Scout

After a crazy few days, it seemed like it was Friday before any of us were ready for it. My offer on the house had been accepted, but closing wasn't going to happen until early January so we had time to pack up the house and get that sorted. The agent had listed both my and Marie's places for sale and already had a few people interested in mine, for which I was grateful. I had the money and credit rating to get a mortgage on the new place, but it would be a lot simpler if I could sell the old place before closing and pay for the new house outright. The upside to being an only child was that my folks had gifted me the house when they'd retired down south.

But as much as we'd all been busy during the week, there wasn't anything that was going to distract my girls today. The day I'd been dreading all week. I had no fucking clue how either Marie or Ariel were going to handle saying goodbye to Sarah. I was struggling with my own guilt over what had happened to the poor woman, and I had the added stress that we still hadn't been able to locate that little fucker, Simon, yet. Surely he wouldn't pull shit at a fucking funeral. Would he?

"You both ready to go?"

Marie walked up the hallway with Ariel walking beside her. The little girl was wearing a dark green dress that she'd picked out herself yesterday. It had a mermaid on the bottom of one side of the skirt that had instantly caught her attention when she'd seen it. The material was soft and Ariel hadn't stopped stroking it and rubbing her cheek on it since we bought it. Marie had added black stockings and shoes together with a cute little jacket thing. Winter in Texas wasn't normally too cold, but we'd actually gotten snow last week and the air still held quite a chill, so I was glad to see my girls were rugged up appropriately. Marie looked stunning in a long sleeved, ankle-length, elegant black dress that she'd matched with some sexy, heeled dress boots I couldn't wait to peel off her later. I'd let Marie choose what I wore, and she put me in the black jeans and white shirt from our dinner in Houston. However, today I was wearing my cut over the top of the shirt. Had my holster and gun, too.

"Yeah, let's get moving."

The flat tone of Marie's voice gutted me, but I knew I couldn't fix this shit for her. Today was just something we were all going to have to struggle through. I reached for Ariel and she moved into my arms so I could lift her up against me. With a sniffle, she buried her face against my shoulder as she took a fist full of my beard. I pulled Marie in close and pressed a kiss to her temple.

"C'mon, love."

With a nod, she headed out the door and I followed. Arrow and Nitro were outside, waiting for us on their bikes. They would travel with us to the cemetery where the graveside service was going to be held. They'd keep watch and make sure no one tried anything as we traveled.

It took a little doing, but I eventually got Ariel to release my beard so I could buckle her into her booster seat. I fucking loved how she'd accepted me this past week. She still wasn't talking, but she was a lot more generous with her affection now than she had been. She'd even started instigating hugs with both me and Marie. I was so fucking proud of her with how far she'd already come since we'd pulled her out of that damn ranch house.

The drive to the cemetery was a quiet one, and thankfully it didn't take more than ten minutes to get there. I wanted this day over with already, wanted to move forward with my girls and create happy memories with them. But I knew today had to happen. I was going to have to stand by and watch both my girls cry their hearts out and know there wasn't a damn fucking thing I could do to fix it. Sarah was gone. No one could bring her back.

Marie

I did my best to hold it together throughout the service as Ariel clung to me. Earlier in the week I'd decided not to stand up and speak at the funeral. I could barely think about Sarah without bursting into tears, no way could I stand up and speak to a room full of people about her and not completely break down.

Thankfully, the Chaplin Scout had called in to handle the service was very understanding and hadn't pushed me to do it. He was from up north somewhere, but apparently visited a lot of clubs around southern Texas to perform various ceremonies. I wasn't entirely sure how he fitted into the biker world, but his cut had the Satan's Cowboys insignia on it so I guessed he was one of theirs. And for a man who'd never met Sarah, he did an excellent job of recounting a few memories of her before he prayed for her to have a peaceful crossing to heaven where she'd be free of all pain and worry.

I wanted that for her so much. I'd never given a lot of thought to what happens after you die, but I suddenly found myself praying hard that heaven was real and Sarah was up there enjoying her freedom and watching over us as we continued life here on earth.

Now that the service was over and I stood with Ariel, and with her hand in mine, we moved to stand next to the coffin that had now been lowered into the ground. I gently tossed my pure white rose down on top of the coffin first.

"Your turn, sweetheart."

I'd let Ariel choose whatever flower she'd wanted, and she'd picked a big sunflower for her mom. She leaned forward and dropped the bloom on top of mine, staring at it the entire time. I swiped the tears away as I tried desperately to not start sobbing. Ariel needed me to be strong.

The Chaplin came to stand next to me for a few minutes.

"You know, Marie, it's perfectly okay to cry. To let Ariel see you cry for your sister. It shows her it's okay for her to grieve too. Society tells us we need to stay stoic and strong for our children, but in reality, they need to see us be weak sometimes. So they know it's okay to have emotions and to release them."

His words cracked my shell wide open and sobs tore from my throat. Ariel turned and buried her face against me and her little body shook as she too sobbed her heart out. Instinctively I knew it was Scout I sensed coming up behind me and I lifted Ariel up against me, before turning to bury my face against his chest. He wrapped his arms around the pair of us, and after pressing a kiss to the top of each of our heads, just stood there holding us as we both cried for Sarah.

Eventually the storm passed, and after a few final sniffles I pulled back from him. I tilted my head up and he took the invitation and leaned down to give me a sweet kiss on the lips. He then handed me a tissue with a small smile and I used it to wipe my eyes. Ariel was clinging to me but her body wasn't shaking any more.

"Ariel? Sweetheart?" She lifted her face and I wiped her eyes before stroking my knuckles over her reddened cheek. "Are you ready to go?"

She wriggled to get down so I lowered her till she stood beside me again. She walked up to the gravesite and my heart split in two when she kneeled down in the dirt beside her mother's grave. I could see her mouth moving, but couldn't hear her quiet words from where I stood. No child should have to say good bye to a parent so young. It was wrong on so many levels.

A lot of the other club members who'd come to support us had moved on to the clubhouse already, where we were holding a wake of sorts, but that could wait. No way would I rush this. Ariel needed to say goodbye, and if this is how she wanted to do it, then she could take all the time in the world to finish it. Scout was by my side, with his arm wrapped around me, his palm rubbing up and down my arm. I realized in that moment that he truly was my everything. My shelter, my protector, my home. Now that he'd finally woken up and claimed me, I knew he'd always be there for me, always be willing to do whatever it took to give me what I needed or wanted.

After several minutes, Ariel stood on wobbly legs and took a step toward us. Scout, seeing her struggling, rushed forward to pick her up. He lifted her high so she could look to me over her shoulder. Suddenly her teary red eyes widened, her body stiffened and she screamed out loud for the first time.

"No! Look out!"

Ignoring the shock of her actually speaking, I spun around just in time to raise my hands and shove aside the arm of the scrawny looking man who had been about to grab me. In that moment, I was so grateful that Zara had convinced me to go with her to a few of Mac's self-defense classes down at the gym.

"Fucking bitch. Come 'ere."

"Like hell."

Wrapping the straps of my handbag around my fingers, I was ready when he lunged at me a second time. I swung the bag up as hard and fast as I could, thankful I'd loaded all sorts of stuff in there for today. The thing weighed half a ton. It connected with the front of his face and he went down to the ground, cupping his now bleeding nose as he groaned.

With a growl, Scout all but threw Ariel into my arms as he drew his weapon from the holster on his belt. He kicked the man over onto his back, and with one boot on the center of his chest, he waited for him to look up at him. I pressed Ariel's face against my chest so she couldn't see what was going to happen.

"Hello, Simon. We meet again. Didn't my boys explain to you what would happen if you tried to come after us?"

"You murdered my brother!"

"Bullshit. He was executed for his crimes. Your bastard of a brother was one of the men who helped make the drug Bruce gave to Sarah. He was also one of the ones who used Sarah while she was fucking high on that shit. He got what he deserved. Just as you will."

The only response Scout got to that declaration was a groan.

"Did you think I was gonna fucking let you walk away after you tried to blow up my woman's house with her and me inside the damn place? And what the fuck were you gonna do here today if my woman hadn't kicked your ass?"

"Return the favor. You took from me, I'm gonna take from you."

Scout laughed darkly. "Like hell you will."

He'd planned on killing me? Right here in front of Ariel and Scout? Bile churned and rose up my throat but I fought to keep it down. Nitro and Arrow came running across the cemetery and when they reached us, Scout took his foot off the bastard who had caused us so much trouble.

"Take him. You know where. No need to be gentle about it. I'll be seeing you later for another lesson in why you don't fuck with Charon MC, Simon. This one will definitely make a *permanent* impression."

For a minute Scout stood completely still as he watched his brothers drag the now sobbing man away. Then Ariel snuffled against me. The sound seemed to snap Scout out of his stupor. He holstered his gun and stepped up to us. His gaze ran over me from head to toe.

"Did he hurt you?"

I shook my head. "No, thanks to Ariel warning me, I turned in time to knock his arm away."

His body sagged with relief for a moment before he wrapped his arms around us both and pressed a kiss to the top of Ariel's head, then my mouth.

"Thank you, Ariel. You saved Marie's life just now by calling out. I can never thank you enough."

A new rush of tears filled my eyes when she turned her face up to Scout and whispered to him.

"Don't cry, Papa. Mommy's okay now."

My heart bloomed with warmth and shattered at the same time. I had no idea when she'd decided to call us those names, and as much as I loved her for it, I didn't want her to think I was trying to replace Sarah.

"Ariel, I'd love to be your mommy, but I don't want to replace your momma. Does that make sense?"

She shook her little head. "My momma is gone to heaven now, she'll watch me from there, and you'll be my mommy who'll watch me from here."

Out of the mouths of babes. Speechless, I pressed a kiss to her temple and looked up to Scout's face to see that Ariel had been right, there were tears running down my big, tough biker's face.

"I love you both more than life itself. Now let's get to the clubhouse before anything else can jump out at us, or all the others eat all the good food."

I smiled and had to chuckle. His voice was gruff and he was clearly trying to change the subject to something lighter. Although, he did have a valid point. Those boys could pack away a serious amount of food.

"Okay, okay, we're moving."

Ariel reached for Scout and he took her from me. As much as I loved holding her, she was heavy to carry while walking across uneven ground like that of the cemetery. Scout held her easily with one arm and wrapped the other around my shoulders as we made our way back to the car. As sad and traumatic as today had been, I couldn't help but feel content now it was over. I had my family. My man by my side and a daughter in his arms for us both to love and cherish.

The future, for once, looked bright.

Epilogue

Saturday, one week later.
Scout

After handing Bulldog a glass of whiskey, I sat down at my desk in my office at the clubhouse.

"So, today's the day huh?"

I nodded to one of my closest friends and VP. "Yep. It is."

Running a palm over the leather vest that sat spread out over my desk, I had to grin. Today I was going to put my property patch on my woman, along with a ring on her finger.

"See? Aren't you glad you listened to me and pulled your head out of your ass? Just a pity you didn't do it years ago."

I winced. "No need to rub that shit in, brother. I know I was a fool, but I wised up before it was too late. She's all fucking mine now, and we've got Ariel to raise. We're looking forward, not back."

Bulldog nodded as he took another drink. "Good deal. When is she getting here?"

I'd had to come down early to deal with some club business, but Marie was arriving any minute now with Ariel for the family barbecue we were having today.

"Any time now."

"Ah, well, I'll get out of here and make sure she finds her way straight to you while we occupy little Ariel out in the yard."

That had me grinning as Bulldog finished his drink and left the room. Ariel had started talking more. She still wasn't a chatterbox like most little girls, but she at least was comfortable telling us what she needed now. And she'd grown rather protective of little Cleo. Since I knew Eagle and Silk were out in the yard with the adorable Cleo, I knew I was going to be able to have some private time with my old lady when she got here.

Before long there was a light tap on the door. I went over to open it and my jaw just about dropped open at what I found.

"Marie?"

With a nervous laugh she did a little spin. "You don't like it?"

"I fucking love it. Get in here."

I tugged her inside and slammed my door, flipping the lock. Before I could get her pinned up against the thing, she wriggled away from me and strolled over to the desk, giving me a great fucking view of her ass swaying in her short, black leather skirt. *Fuck me.*

"Is this for me?"

Finally I managed to pull my gaze from her ass and saw that she was stroking her cut.

"Yep, it's all yours, babe. You'll be the only woman I ever offer it to. You gonna wear my property patch for me?"

She glanced over her shoulder at me. "Of course I will."

When she went to pick it up, I stopped her. "Hold up." Before she could comment, I gripped the bottom of her shirt and pulled it over her head, then unclipped her bra. Once she was naked from the waist up, I took her cut and put it on her. She didn't say a word, but the smirk she wore told me she knew what I wanted.

"Now that's a sight I'm never gonna forget."

Tight leather skirt that ended mid-thigh, topped with her leather cut. All in matching black leather. She was a walking wet dream built specifically for me. I ran my palms up her sides and kneaded her tits for a few moments before I tweaked her nipples. Unable to resist a moment longer, I crashed my mouth over hers, kissing her deeply as I pulled her close before lifting her so she sat on the desk. She spread her thighs for me and when I put my hands back on her tits, she went to work on my pants. I pulled from the kiss to groan when she released my cock from my jeans and wrapped a hand around it to start stroking.

"Fuck, babe."

Needing inside her, I moved her hand off me, shoved her skirt up as I tugged her forward so she was sitting right on the edge of the desk. Shoving her panties to the side, I lined up my cock with her wet entrance and slid home.

"Oh, Charlie. So good."

I hadn't planned on fucking her this early on, but the damn woman had distracted me wearing a short fucking skirt that gave me easy access. Not that I was complaining. I could do the other thing after I'd finished taking care of her, and I would never, ever turn down a chance to be inside my love.

I leaned her back over the desk before I gripped her hips and started fucking her in earnest. Watching her lush tits bounce under her cut, her tight little nipples peeking out beside the front patch that declared her as mine had my balls tightening up long before I was ready for this to be over. I shifted my hand so I could tease her clit with my thumb as I pumped into her.

"Fuck, babe. Love you so fucking much."

She smiled, then groaned and arched her back as I hit her g-spot.

"Love you too. Don't stop."

"Never. I'll never fucking stop loving you, Marie."

On my final word, she came, her pussy clamping down on my cock and pulling my come from me. I leaned down over her to rest for a moment as I caught my breath. Before I crushed her under my weight, I moved to stand, sliding out of her heat. Her panties slid back into place, covering her pussy and keeping my come inside her as I tucked myself back in my jeans and buttoned up.

"Fuck, babe. You make me lose my head."

I reached over and snagged a handful of tissues and wiped her thighs clean before I pulled her up so she was sitting. She was looking adorable and a little shell-shocked, so I kissed her again until she was moaning into my mouth.

I took a step back, slipped the ring from my pocket and dropped to my knee in front of her.

"Marie, baby, will you make me the luckiest man alive and marry me?"

Tears filled her eyes instantly and she jumped down off the desk. Her bouncing tits were distracting, but not as distracting as the fact she hadn't answered me yet. I was starting to get nervous when she dropped down in front of me.

"Yes, a hundred times yes. I love you so much, Charlie. I'd love nothing more than to be your wife."

Relief washed over me. She'd scared the shit out of me there with the hesitation and tears before she answered. I slid the ring onto her finger. I'd gone with a simple solitaire diamond in a design that was flat enough she'd be able to wear it with bike gloves on.

"I have a present for you, too."

She stood and grabbed her bag from the floor near the door where she'd dropped it, and dug around for a minute. Curious, I stood and followed behind her.

"What have you done?"

"Well, this was what we both did." She turned around and handed me a long piece of plastic that had two blue lines in the clear window in the center.

"A pregnancy test? You're— We're pregnant? For real?"

My heart felt like it was gonna burst out of my chest.

"Yeah, Papa. We're pregnant. Only a couple weeks at the most."

Well, duh, they'd only been fucking like rabbits for a few weeks.

"Get dressed, we gotta go tell everyone. Fuck, this is the best news ever. I love you so fucking much, babe."

I kissed her again, long and deep, before I released her long enough to get dressed. I was still staring at the two little lines that were going to upend my world when she came back to stand in front of me.

"Come on then, let's go tell the family our news."

That had me grinning even wider. "Well, I did promise you a family, babe. Can't ever say I didn't keep that promise. You got a daughter, another baby on the way and a whole heap of brothers and sisters to boot."

She rolled her eyes on a laugh before she cupped my face in her palms and gave me the sweetest kiss I'd ever had. My hands crept down her legs to hook under her skirt.

Fuck the family. They could wait another half hour to find out our news.

Other Charon MC Books:

Book 1:
Inking Eagle

The sins of her father will be her undoing… unless a hero rides to her rescue.

As the 15th anniversary of the 9/11 attacks nears, Silk struggles to avoid all reminders of the day she was orphaned. She's working hard in her tattoo shop, Silky Ink, and working even harder to keep her eyes and her hands off her bodyguard, Eagle. She'd love to forget her sorrows in his strong arms.

But Eagle is a prospect in the Charon MC, and her uncle is the VP. As a Daughter of the Club, she's off limits to the former Marine. But not for long. As soon as he patches in, he intends to claim Silk for his old lady. He'll wear her ink, and she'll wear his patch.

Too late, they learn that Silk's father had dark secrets, ones that have lived beyond his grave. When demons from the past come for Silk, Eagle will need all the skills he learned in the Marines to get his woman back safe, and keep her that way.

Book 2:
Fighting Mac

*She's no sleeping beauty, but then he's no prince -
just a biker warrior to the rescue.*

For the past three years Claire 'Zara' Flynn has been at the mercy of narcolepsy and cataplexy attacks. But after she witnesses a shooting by the ruthless Iron Hammers MC, her problems get a whole lot worse. She's now a marked woman, on the run for her life.

Former Marine Jacob 'Mac' Miller has a good life with the Charon MC. He works in the club gym and teaches self-defense classes - in the hopes of saving other women from the violent death his sister suffered. When the pretty new waitress at a local cafe catches his attention, he wants her in his bed. But there's a problem. She's clearly scared of all bikers. Wanting to help her, he talks her into coming to his class. Mac soon realizes he wants to keep her close in more ways than one. But can he, when his club's worst enemies come after her?

When Zara disappears, Mac and his brothers must go to war to get her back. Because this time, she wakes up in a terrible place... surrounded by other desperate women, and guarded by the Iron Hammers MC. Can her leather-clad prince ride to the rescue in time to save her from hell?

Book 3:
Chasing Taz

He lived his life one conquest at a time. She calculated her every move… until she met him.

Former Marine Donovan 'Taz' Lee might appear to be a carefree Aussie bloke living it up as a member of the Texan motorcycle club, Charon MC, but the truth is so much more complicated. With blood and tears haunting his past and threatening to destroy his future, Taz is completely unprepared for the woman of his dreams, when she comes in and knocks him on his ass. Literally.

Felicity "Flick" Vaughn joined the FBI to get answers behind her brother's dishonorable discharge and abandonment of his family. Knowing Taz was a part of her brother's final mission, she agrees to partner with him to go after a bigger club, The Satan's Cowboys MC.

However, nothing in life is ever simple and Flick is totally unprepared to have genuine feelings for the sexy

Aussie. When secrets are revealed and their worlds are busted wide open, will they be strong enough to still be standing when the dust settles?

Book 4:
Claiming Tiny

Some rules were meant to be broken.

After being raised in foster care, Ryan 'Tiny' Nelson has no plans to settle down. But that idea goes right out the window when Missy shows up at the clubhouse. One taste of the Charon MC's newest club whore and he's hooked.

Love is the last thing on Mercedes 'Missy' Soto's mind when she runs to the Charon MC for protection. But the first time Tiny wraps his arms around her, he captures her heart in the process.

When things start unravelling, Missy panics and runs. Will Tiny find her in time to give her a Christmas to remember, or will he lose her forever once her past catches up with her?

223

225

227

229